No one noticed that
the sand was getting softer and softer,
not even Paddlefoot.

Without warning, the big dinosaur sank up to his hips in quicksand!

Magnolia screamed as he went down. Paddlefoot trumpeted in terror and tried to get out But the more he struggled, the deeper he sank into tne treacherous quicksand. Magnolia could barely hang on.

"Stop! Stop!" she cried. "That's not working! You're just getting us *deeper!*"

"I know!" wailed the Lambeosaurus. He was now up to his thick waist in the soggy sand.

"Just stay calm," ordered Magnolia, trying to sound calm herself. She looked around and saw that the pool of quicksand was too wide for her to jump over and get help.

Then Magnolia began to have an even greater fear than her fear of drowning. They were at the edge of the Rainy Basin—and that was Tyrannosaurus rex territory!

VISIT THE EXCITING WORLD OF

IN THESE BOOKS:

Windchaser by Scott Ciencin

River Quest by John Vornholt

AND COMING IN FALL 1995:

Hatchling by Midori Snyder

Lost City by Scott Ciencin

DINOTOPIA®
RIVER QUEST

by John Vornholt

BULLSEYE BOOKS

Random House New York

For my Dad
—J.V.

Special thanks to
paleontologist Michael Brett-Surman, Ph.D.,
James Gurney, and Scott Usher.

A BULLSEYE BOOK PUBLISHED BY RANDOM HOUSE, INC.

Copyright © 1995 by James Gurney
Cover art copyright © 1995 by James Gurney
All rights reserved under International and Pan-American Copyright Conventions.
Published in the United States by Random House, Inc., New York,
and simultaneously by Random House of Canada Limited, Toronto.
Based on *Dinotopia*® by James Gurney,
published in 1992 by Turner Publishing, Inc., Atlanta.
All rights reserved.

Library of Congress Catalog Card Number: 95-67148

ISBN: 0-679-86982-4

RL: 5.6

Manufactured in the United States of America 10 9 8 7 6 5 4 3 2 1

DINOTOPIA IS A REGISTERED TRADEMARK OF THE GREENWICH WORKSHOP, INC.,
© 1992 JAMES GURNEY

Cover illustration by Michael Welpley

RIVER QUEST

Windy Point

Crystal Caverns •

The Hatchery •

Baz •••

Pooktook •

NORTHERN PLAINS

CRACKSHELL POINT

Cornucopia •
Treetown • • Deep Lake
• Bent Root

Volcaneum •

Palongo River

Temple Ruins ••

BACKBONE MOUNTAINS

Rocky Pass   Prosperine •

Sapphire Bay

• Poseidos
(sunken)

*Hadro
Swamp*

Waterfall City •

R A I N Y

B A S I N

GREAT CANAL

SKY GALLEY CAVES •

Arna River

Pteros •

Warmwater
Bay

Culebra •

FORBIDDEN MOUNTAINS

Canyon City •

Tentpole of the Sky •

Sculpted Cliffs ••

Sky City •

Thermala •

Ancient Gorge

The Sentinels

GREAT DESERT

OUTER ISLAND

The Time Towers •

*Red Rapid
Canyon*

The Portal

• Sauropolis

Dolphin Bay

• Chandara

B L A C K W O O D

F L A T S

Dragonfly Coast

Cape Turtletail

CHAPTER 1

A spray of scalding water hit Magnolia in the face, and she threw up one hand to ward it off. She didn't need to tell Paddlefoot to back up. The Lambeosaurus pivoted gracefully, for a creature weighing six tons and standing twenty feet tall. Thirteen-year-old Magnolia just hung on for the ride.

Paddlefoot jogged several yards on his hind legs, then halted. Both of them looked back at the towering spume of water. The geyser shot a thousand feet into the air, like an upside-down waterfall, and it turned the valley into a steam bath. Magnolia couldn't hear anything over the hiss of the steam, and she could smell the sulfur.

She felt the presence of her master, Edwick, as he thundered to her side aboard his partner, Calico, a spotted Saltasaurus. She was relieved to see their yellow, green, and white colors, and the water lily on Calico's blanket. Edwick and Calico were the Habitat Partners of Freshwater, and Magnolia and Paddlefoot were their apprentices.

"Report?" asked Edwick, who was an old man and didn't like to waste words on things like greetings.

"Yes, sir!" shouted Magnolia, over the noise of the geyser. "We watched it for two hours, but it just erupted a moment ago. It's even bigger than we were told!"

Edwick rubbed his short white beard and stared at the amazing sight. "It's beautiful! But a new geyser could mean that earthquakes or problems with underground water channels are coming. It usually means there are old volcanoes somewhere close."

"Volcaneum is nearby," Paddlefoot pointed out, trying to be helpful. The dinosaur's voice was a series of hoots and bellows produced by his hornlike crest. Most humans couldn't understand him, but Magnolia and Edwick had spent years with Paddlefoot. They understood him perfectly.

Edwick motioned around the small but perfect valley deep in the forest. "This whole area is a sunken volcano. I was going to recommend this area for farming, but I don't think so now!"

Without warning, the geyser shut off. The spume that had been a thousand feet high dropped down to a little squirt of steam. Finally, they could talk without shouting.

"Maybe it's blown itself out," said Edwick. "The larger the geyser, the quicker it can blow itself out. Make note of that, Apprentice."

"Yes, sir," Magnolia answered, knowing she would

never forget it. "And why is that true, sir?"

Edwick smiled. "A good apprentice always asks 'why.' Imagine what is happening. Water collects in a series of underground chambers, where it's heated by molten rock. The water turns into steam. It expands and expands until it has nowhere to go, except for this little hole in the rock. Then it *explodes!*"

When Magnolia jumped at his words, the old man laughed. "It shouldn't explode again until the water collects and reheats. If enough water has blown out, it might never explode again. So that is why, the more water the geyser shoots, the shorter its life usually is."

"Never thought of that," said Paddlefoot.

Edwick reached into the backpack on his saddle and pulled out a long coil of rope. There were black stripes all along the rope, and one end had a large weight tied to it.

"We should take a measurement to see how deep the water is in the top chamber," he said. "I want to know how fast it's collecting. It could tell us if this will be a long-lived or a short-lived geyser. Wait here."

"Sir," said Magnolia with concern, "you shouldn't get too close!"

"Didn't you say you watched it for two hours before it erupted? This will take only a few minutes. Back up a bit, take out your spyglass, and observe me. Are you ready, Calico?"

For fifty feet around, all the greenery and dirt had

been blown away by the powerful forces of the geyser. Paddlefoot moved well beyond the clearing, and Magnolia fumbled in her saddlebag for her spyglass. She extended the small telescope and put it to her eye just in time to see Calico and Edwick arrive at the silent geyser.

She bit her lip nervously as she watched Edwick dismount from Calico and walk toward the geyser on his bowed legs. Edwick and Calico had spent many years patrolling the lakes, rivers, streams, and swamps of Dinotopia. It was their job to monitor all the freshwater on the island, including geysers.

Edwick swung the weighted rope as if he hadn't a care in the world, and Magnolia began to relax. Edwick and Calico were always very careful, she told herself. That was why both had lived to such a ripe old age.

When Edwick began to lower the weighted rope into the water, Magnolia concentrated on how he was doing it. Through the spyglass, which was a good one given to her by her father, she could see his lips moving as he counted off the marks on the rope. Because the geyser had frightened off most of the birds and small animals, it was extremely quiet in this part of the forest. She could hear her heart beating.

"Something's wrong," said Paddlefoot in a hushed bellow.

"What?" asked Magnolia. "It's quiet, that's all."

"Too quiet," snorted Paddlefoot. Without being

able to help himself, the huge Lambeosaurus began to shift around on his mammoth hind legs. His padded front feet pawed the ground too.

"Will you hold still!" demanded Magnolia. "I can't see anything."

Then the earthquake hit! It sounded like thunder, and turned the ground into a rolling carnival ride. The sure-footed Lambeosaurus staggered but didn't lose his balance. Somehow Magnolia managed to stay in her saddle and not drop her spyglass. The quake lasted less than a minute, but it seemed as if they stumbled around helplessly for hours.

When it finally stopped, the geyser erupted again!

"No!" screamed Magnolia. She touched Paddle-foot's thick neck, and the crested dinosaur leaped forward.

Magnolia shielded her eyes as they rode into a mist of steaming water. She hadn't been watching Edwick and Calico when the earthquake struck and the geyser erupted, so she didn't know what had happened to them. Now she couldn't see them for the thick haze of steam!

Paddlefoot nearly ran into Calico, who was backing up and craning her neck to see through the mist. The Saltasaurus made distressed gliding sounds in her throat, and Magnolia knew perfectly well what she was saying: "Edwick is hurt! Help him!"

The thirteen-year-old grabbed a coil of rope from her saddlebag and leaped off the Lambeosaurus.

"Hold still," she shouted at Paddlefoot as she dashed between his mammoth legs. Using the dinosaur's body as shelter from the scalding water, she peered into the steam.

That was when she saw Edwick, a pathetic lump, trying to crawl out of the roaring steam.

"I found him!" she told the dinosaurs. "Paddlefoot, catch!" She tossed one end of her rope to the dinosaur, who deftly caught it in his mouth.

Then she rushed forward with the rest of the rope. She shielded her eyes and protected herself as best she could, but she felt the boiling water sear her skin. If she was getting burned, she thought with alarm, what must be happening to Edwick? He was in the middle of it!

When Magnolia couldn't get any closer, she uncoiled the rope.

"Catch!" she shouted at the injured man, hoping he could hear her.

There might not be another chance if she missed, so she threw the rope with all the strength and accuracy she could muster. It landed just inches in front of him.

"Grab it!" she shouted. "Grab it!"

With his last bit of strength, the old man lunged forward and got his gnarled hands around the rope.

"Pull!" she shouted to Paddlefoot. "Slowly!"

The rope began to move, and she stared with

fright into the steam to make sure Edwick was holding on. *He was!*

"Hang on!" she encouraged him. "You're almost out of it!"

She tried not to think of the pain Edwick was suffering as Paddlefoot dragged him out of the steaming water. When the old man drew close to her, she reached under his arms and helped him hang on. When she touched his skin, she felt the blisters. Even his white beard had been scorched off. Nevertheless, Edwick held on to the rope, and Paddlefoot kept pulling him to safety.

Moments later, they were out of the worst of it, although the geyser kept spitting water a thousand feet into the air.

"Edwick!" moaned Calico. The dinosaur nuzzled him with her big snout. He had used his last bit of strength to hold on to the rope, and now the old man was unconscious.

Magnolia tried to be brave, but one glance at Edwick's blistered skin told her how serious his injuries were. "He's badly burned. We must get him to Volcaneum as soon as possible."

Calico snorted something to Paddlefoot, and the two dinosaurs craned their long necks to the ground and wriggled their snouts under Edwick. They lifted him up as if he were a feather pillow and placed him gently into his saddle aboard Calico. Magnolia scrambled up with her rope and tied him into his seat. When she was done, she jumped down.

"Be gentle, but go quickly," she told Calico. "We will meet you at Volcaneum." Then the big Saltasaurus took off at a brisk, steady walk, careful not to shake her wounded passenger.

Magnolia gulped back tears. Edwick could be brusque with her, and sometimes he treated her like a child. But she was barely a teenager, and she had so much to learn from him! Please let him be all right, she begged the fates. Please let Master Edwick live!

"Let's follow them," said Magnolia. She tried to climb aboard Paddlefoot, but her hands slipped. She yelped with pain and became aware of her own blisters and burn spots. With their thick hides, the dinosaurs had barely been affected by the scalding water.

"You're not well either!" the Lambeosaurus bellowed with concern. "Let me help you." The big hadrosaur spread himself out on his belly to make it as easy as possible for Magnolia to climb onto his back.

"Thanks," said the girl. She felt sick, but she didn't know whether it was her burns or her worry over Edwick. She touched the dinosaur's neck, and he rose to his feet and gently walked forward.

With her blistered hands, Magnolia couldn't use the reins. So she wrapped her arms around Paddlefoot's neck and hung on. She knew the journey would take at least four or five hours.

The city of Volcaneum sat atop a stubby mountain

that had once been an active volcano. Now it was a manufacturing center, and the thermal energy from deep within the earth helped to forge jewelry, tools, hinges, all kinds of metal goods. There were small villages surrounding the base of the mountain, and Magnolia and Paddlefoot headed into the nearest one.

Word spread fast on Dinotopia, and human and dinosaur nurses came rushing out to greet Magnolia and Paddlefoot. The Lambeosaurus knelt down on his front legs, and the nurses lifted the thirteen-year-old off and carried her into a white hut with a thatched roof. Paddlefoot clucked his tongue with concern.

"What about Edwick?" asked Magnolia. "What about Edwick?"

"He is resting, as you should be," said one of the nurses. "His burns are worse, but yours are bad, too." She turned to a Protoceratops nurse. "Let's have the longevus salve. Quickly!"

While the dinosaur went to fetch the medicine, the human nurses lay Magnolia in a bed and began to strip off her dirty clothes. By the time the Protoceratops arrived with the salve, Magnolia was already starting to drift off to sleep.

"Edwick," she muttered. "I want to see my master."

"You will, my dear," cooed the nurse. "First you must rest. Rest is the most important thing now."

CHAPTER 2

When Magnolia awoke, it was dark except for a small lamp, and she felt confused by her surroundings. This wasn't her bed! Where was she? The smell of fresh bread was comforting, but there were jarring noises— a bell ringing, the clacking of wagon wheels on the street.

Magnolia started to get up, and stabs of pain along her skin reminded her of what had happened. She touched her face and found that her burns were covered with salve and bandages. Now she remembered— she was in a village outside Volcaneum.

She lay back in bed, trying to calm herself. She actually wasn't hurt that badly, but what about Edwick? How was he? She just had to know.

"Nurse!" she shouted. "Nurse!"

The little Protoceratops hustled into the room, rose up on her hind legs, and chattered at Magnolia to be quiet. The girl obeyed, knowing there wasn't any point in arguing with a Protoceratops. She lay still, hoping somebody would come to visit her soon and

10

answer the questions that crowded her mind.

Luckily, Magnolia didn't have long to wait, and when somebody did come, it was an important somebody. The muscular body of Tok Timbu filled the doorway, the lamplight glinting off his bald head. He was the master metalworker, the most important human in Volcaneum.

"Are you awake?" he asked in a thunderous voice.

"Yes, sir," Magnolia answered meekly. "I didn't mean to cause a problem."

"There is no problem," said Tok Timbu, stroking his long white beard. "You want to see Edwick, and he wishes to see you as soon as possible. Can you walk, or shall I carry you?"

"I can walk," she said, swinging her legs out of bed. Her burns were painful, but they were only on her hands and face. Her clothes had protected the rest of her body. The nurses had left slippers and a soft robe for her, all of which she slipped on.

"Come then," said Tok Timbu. He was so big and Magnolia was so short, only five feet tall, that she felt as if she were walking beside a dinosaur.

They stepped outside into a deserted street of white cottages and flickering lampposts. The government buildings and foundries were at the top of the volcano, with this sleepy village that housed the workers right below. It was late at night, and she must have slept a long time.

"Is Master Edwick all right?" asked Magnolia,

trotting to keep up with the metalworker.

He nodded. "As well as can be expected with burns all over his body. He will live, but he will be healing for a long time."

"But the habitat?" asked Magnolia. "Who will check the freshwater?"

Tok Timbu smiled. "That is why we must talk." He stopped outside a white cottage and tapped the door knocker. A moment later, a human nurse answered the door.

She bowed and looked from the muscular man to Magnolia. "He is awake, but please do not stay long."

"This is urgent business," said Tok Timbu. He ushered Magnolia inside the cottage. There were three patients sleeping in the living room, but the nurse directed them toward a back bedroom.

When they entered, Magnolia was relieved to find that the room was dimly lit by a single lamp, and she couldn't see Edwick's wounds clearly. But there was no mistaking the gruff voice.

"Magnolia," he said fondly. "Thanks to you, I live to see another day."

She knelt beside Edwick's bed and reached out to touch his arm. Then, worried about his burns, she put her hands on the bed railing instead.

Edwick looked so old and frail, not the dynamic man she had followed from one end of Dinotopia to another. For five years, Edwick had been her mother, father, friend, and teacher. She knew he wasn't going to die, but she had to fight back tears just seeing him like this.

"Did Tok tell you why I wanted to see you?"

"No," she answered, "but I wanted to see you, anyway."

Edwick tried to smile, but bandages hid most of his face. "Congratulations, little Magnolia, your apprenticeship is over."

"What?" she gasped.

"You and Paddlefoot are the new Habitat Partners of Freshwater. At this moment, Calico is meeting with Paddlefoot and the elder dinosaurs."

"No!" Magnolia groaned. "I'm not ready! I'm too young!"

Edwick croaked a laugh. "Look at *me*. You're more ready than I am. You warned me not to go near that geyser, but I went anyway. When the apprentice has more sense than the master, it is time for the master to retire."

Magnolia started to protest again, but Edwick held up a bandaged hand. "You and Paddlefoot have apprenticed for five long years. You are ready. What you lack in experience, you make up for in youth.

"You must leave tomorrow morning for Waterfall City—to study the old maps and to talk to Malik and Nallab. I am worried about that earthquake. It may have an effect on water levels or water quality."

"I'm worried too," said Magnolia, "but that doesn't mean I'm ready to be a Habitat Partner."

Tok Timbu laid his massive hand on her shoulder. "Do not argue, young one. It is the master's decision to say when the apprentice is ready. Of course, the official ceremony that makes you and Paddlefoot the protectors of freshwater will have to wait for another time."

"She will need a uniform," said Edwick. "Yellow, green, and white."

Tok Timbu nodded. "The villagers are sewing new clothes for her. They will be ready by morning."

Edwick touched Magnolia's arm with his bandaged hand. "Carry the banner of the water lily proudly," he whispered. "And protect the water. It is the lifeblood of Dinotopia."

Magnolia swallowed and bit her lip. She could hardly speak with all the weight of responsibility falling on her slim shoulders. "I will," she promised.

Edwick nodded and lay back in his bed. He seemed to be more at peace than Magnolia had ever seen him. Tok Timbu gently helped the girl to her feet and escorted her out of the room.

When they went outside, they found Paddlefoot waiting for them. He was already wearing Calico's saddle blanket, which was green, yellow, and white, and bore the banner of the water lily. The dinosaur looked every bit as surprised and frightened as Magnolia felt, and she went to hug one of his burly hind legs.

Tok Timbu nodded with satisfaction. "You have been taught by the best. I have no doubt you will do well. I must go now and send word over the crystal beacons. By tomorrow, all of Dinotopia will know that we have new Habitat Partners. Breathe deep and seek peace."

With that, the giant metalworker left them standing in the dark village at the base of the mountain. Paddlefoot made a few plaintive hoots, and Magnolia hugged him again.

"Yes, I know," she said. "We're all alone, and we have a big job ahead of us. I'm scared too."

Magnolia looked toward the top of the mountain, where the forges of Volcaneum burned with an orange glow, lighting the night sky of Dinotopia.

The next morning, Magnolia was delighted to find her new uniform laid out for her. It consisted of a white shirt, green tunic, yellow pantaloons, and—best of all—a hat that matched the crest on Paddlefoot's head! When she put the clothes on, it finally sank in that it was real. She and Paddlefoot really were the Habitat Partners of Freshwater!

She was a bit embarrassed at the send-off the villagers gave them. Of course, Dinotopians didn't need much excuse to celebrate, but an observer would've thought they were going off to save the world. Children and small dinosaurs followed them for miles down the trail, waving and cheering. Magnolia finally had to tell them to go home.

The only sad part was that Edwick wasn't able to

see them off. His nurses wouldn't let him out of his bed, and Magnolia didn't want to see him lying in bed, weak and injured. She wanted to remember him the way he had always been—vibrant and full of action. But Calico came to say good-bye, and that was important to Magnolia and Paddlefoot.

By midday, they were well on their way to Waterfall City. During their apprenticeship, Magnolia and Paddlefoot had traveled every inch of Dinotopia, and they knew every trail and shortcut. Magnolia had a great sense of direction. She often had to tell Edwick and Calico which fork in the road to take.

The only area she didn't know very well was the Rainy Basin. But that was Tyrannosaurus rex territory, and neither dinosaur nor human went there if he could help it.

Magnolia carefully steered them around Hadro Swamp, which lay between Volcaneum and Waterfall City. That added a few miles to their journey, but she didn't want to get stuck in the biggest swamp on Dinotopia, especially traveling alone. They would be spending enough time in the swamp when they went to make their annual inspection.

Even with the detour, it was only about forty miles between Volcaneum and Waterfall City. The Lambeosaurus covered the distance swiftly. Magnolia could tell they were getting close when the terrain changed from lush forest to rocks and rivers. They stopped to rest at a small canyon with a gently flowing river.

She could tell from the mud along the bank that the water level in the river had fallen recently. But there wasn't time to take measurements—they had to reach Waterfall City and see if there were any reports of worse damage.

Paddlefoot hooted, "How about a swim?"

Some hadrosaurs hated to swim, but Paddlefoot liked it, which was a good thing for a Habitat Partner of Freshwater. Waterfall City lay at the junction of several rivers, the greatest being the Polongo. The footpath wound around the mountains, but the river was a direct route.

"Let's go!" she answered.

The dinosaur nodded and plunged happily into the river with the girl clinging to his back. Despite his great bulk, Paddlefoot could paddle with his padded front feet. He could also run under water on his strong hind legs. Paddlefoot and Magnolia had the current to help them, and they were soon moving briskly along.

By late afternoon, they were floating through a vast canyon with striped cliffs rising sharply on both sides of them. They could hear the roar of the great waterfalls from a long way off.

"Do you want to swim all the way in?" asked Magnolia.

"No," honked Paddlefoot. "I'm too tired, and the current is too rough around the waterfalls."

"How about a glider?"

Paddlefoot craned his neck back to look at her, knowing she was joking. There were gliders that zoomed down from the great bluffs overlooking the city, but they were only for humans and small dinosaurs. Creatures the size of Paddlefoot did not fly, nor did they trust boats very much.

"That leaves only the path behind the waterfalls," said Magnolia.

The dinosaur hooted, as if to say that was okay with him.

"Oh, I hate to go that way," muttered the girl. "It's undignified for the new Habitat Partners to arrive soaking wet."

"Says who?" bellowed the Lambeosaurus.

Paddlefoot got his way, and they climbed out of the river before it went cascading into the basin around Waterfall City. Magnolia dismounted and let the dinosaur lead the way—first up to the bluffs, then down a path leading into the waterfalls.

Even though she'd seen Waterfall City a hundred times, she stopped to stare at the magnificent sight. It looked like a castle floating on the edge of the world. The heavy mists gave the buildings a surreal look, as if they were chalk paintings you could wipe away with your hand.

Was it her imagination, or did the mists appear lighter today? The girl could easily make out landmarks that she couldn't always see from here. She saw the golden dome that represented the Earth and housed the Great Spiral Clock. She could also see the pyramids, the library tower, and even the giant statues of long-toothed lions that guarded the river as it flowed through the city.

Even the water level of the mighty Polongo River looked lower today. But it still wasn't low enough to swim in. Waterfall City was her favorite place on Dinotopia; she just wished there was an easier way to get to it.

Magnolia looked longingly at the gliders, shaped like pterosaurs. Each one ferried half a dozen passengers into the city. She also saw several Skybaxes and one-person hang gliders, all of which delivered their passengers to the city in a perfectly dry condition. She wouldn't trade Paddlefoot for any of them, but someday she'd like to *fly* into Waterfall City for a change.

As she stared at the towering waterfalls, she had an overwhelming realization: She and one lone Lambeosaurus were in charge of keeping track of all of this! How could she live up to such a great responsibility? The thought made her want to run in the opposite direction and let somebody else take the job.

Paddlefoot could always sense her moods, and he hooted softly. "Do not be afraid, Magnolia. We can do it."

She shook her head. "I don't know. I worry too much. Even now, it looks to me as if the water level of the Polongo River is low today. Is that possible?"

"Come on!" snorted Paddlefoot, tromping down a

path that led to the mouth of a giant cave.

Before she even reached the cave, Magnolia was drenched and shivering. The mist was so thick near the cave that she had to breathe through her mouth instead of her nose. She hoped that it wouldn't be too slippery inside.

After her eyes got used to the darkness, Magnolia relaxed a bit. They were in a deep cavern that wandered directly behind the waterfall created by the Polongo River. Although it was a damp form of travel, walking behind a waterfall was still rather exciting.

Ahead of her, Paddlefoot had to be careful to avoid stalactites hanging from the ceiling and stalagmites rising from the floor. They were caused by the mist condensing and dripping though cracks in the rock, leaving minerals behind.

The noise of the plunging water reminded her of where they were. Between the stalactites and stalagmites, she could see the waterfall. From behind, it looked like a shimmering turquoise curtain, not tons of water plummeting hundreds of feet per second.

As they walked farther, she began to see gaps in the curtain of water, gaps which had never been there before. She could even hear Paddlefoot's heavy footsteps sloshing through the puddles. In their many trips behind the waterfall, she had never heard any sounds but the roar of the water. What was going on?

"Look!" she told Paddlefoot. "There's something wrong with the river!"

CHAPTER 3

The Lambeosaurus turned to look at what should have been a solid sheet of water. Instead there were huge gaps in the waterfall. In some places, it was only a trickle.

He snorted. "Did they divert the river?"

Magnolia could only shrug. She knew that every hundred years or so, the citizens of Waterfall City had to divert the Polongo River to rebuild the cliffs. It had never happened in her lifetime.

"Would they divert a river without telling the Habitat Partners?" she asked. If she knew Edwick and Calico, they would want to oversee such a complicated process.

"I don't know," hooted Paddlefoot. Nevertheless, the dinosaur quickened his pace, and Magnolia had to run to keep up with him.

When they emerged on the other side of the cave, they had to climb several steps to reach the outer wall of the city. Even before they got to the wall, they could hear the cries and shouts from within. Nobody was even watching the gate when they entered.

The city was in chaos! Humans were running around, shouting and pointing; dinosaurs were stamping and bellowing. Dragonhorns sounded from the highest towers, and alarm bells rang. Humans and dinosaurs were rushing up to the walls of the city, trying to get a better look.

"The river!" someone shouted. "It's drying up!"

"What is happening?" wailed a Stegosaurus.

"Let's ask Nallab! He will know!"

Magnolia and Paddlefoot passed a large fountain that had stopped working for lack of water. Suddenly, they were spotted by the panicked crowd.

"The new Habitat Partners of Freshwater!" a woman screamed. "They will tell us!"

Within seconds, the young Habitat Partners were mobbed by worried citizens.

"Why is the water level dropping? What is happening? Tell us! Tell us!" they all shouted at once.

To keep from being swallowed up by the crowd, Magnolia quickly scrambled aboard Paddlefoot. "Remain calm!" she yelled at the top of her voice, not knowing what else to say.

Her main concern was the Great Spiral Clock. It wasn't a clock that kept minutes and hours—it was used to tell the time for planting, harvesting, and egg hatching. Unlike other cities on Dinotopia, Waterfall City was totally dependent upon waterwheels for power. When the water level dropped too much, everything stopped.

If a milling machine or a spinning wheel stopped turning, it wasn't so serious. But if the Spiral Clock stopped turning, all of Dinotopia would suffer.

"I must go see Malik!" she told the crowd.

This managed to calm them a little, as if something were being done. Magnolia was only thirteen years old, but she knew that Dinotopians placed a lot of faith in the Habitat Partners. The people didn't see her age—they saw only the banner of the water lily.

She urged Paddlefoot forward through the crowded streets. They passed dried canals, dried fountains, and giant waterwheels that had stopped turning. Without water flowing through it, Waterfall City was a ghost of itself, like a town that had been deserted.

They climbed the steps to the Time Door, just as Malik poked his head out. Malik was a thin Stenonychosaurus, hardly much bigger than Magnolia, but as timekeeper he kept the pulse of Dinotopia. He waved frantically to them.

"Come in! Come in!"

Magnolia leaped down and entered the small door, and Paddlefoot continued around the corner to enter a huge door built especially for large dinosaurs.

Malik hurried the girl through the Time Museum.

She'd always enjoyed seeing his collection of curious timepieces, carried ashore by newcomers from all over the world. But there was no time to look at them today. Malik and Magnolia reached the dome that housed the Spiral Clock just as Paddlefoot entered from the other side.

As in the rest of the city, the river level had fallen so low that water had stopped flowing through the sluice that turned the waterwheel. Both it and the Spiral Clock were perfectly still. When it wasn't moving, the giant conelike clock looked like a useless piece of junk instead Dinotopia's greatest invention.

"This is a true disaster!" clucked Malik. "The water level started falling yesterday, after the earthquake. It's getting worse by the hour! Do you know what is happening?"

Magnolia and Paddlefoot could only shake their heads. "We just arrived," said Paddlefoot.

"Oh, yes," said Malik. "Congratulations on your new post. I'm sorry you had to visit us in the middle of a crisis. But I'm glad you're here."

The door banged open, and a tall man with tufts of white hair on his head rushed into the room, his robe flowing behind him. "This is terrible!" he wailed. "Just terrible!"

"Calm yourself, Nallab," said the small dinosaur. "We have a bit of luck—here are the new Habitat Partners of Freshwater."

The old man studied Magnolia and Paddlefoot

and took a few deep breaths. "I am calm now. What do you make of this?"

Magnolia wasn't used to people asking for her opinion. But she and Paddlefoot had wanted this job, they had been trained for it, and now they had it.

"We first saw that the water had dropped when were crossing behind the falls," she answered. "We thought maybe you were diverting the Polongo River to make repairs."

"No," said Nallab. "We do that only after months of preparation and care. We've been sending out teams to check for damage in other towns—we weren't even thinking the river would be damaged! If this keeps up, people will abandon Waterfall City. I don't want it to become like the Lost City!"

"Let's think for a moment," said Magnolia in a calm, grown-up voice. "The earthquake must have done something to divert the river. Can we send Sky-baxes upriver to see what happened?"

Malik shook his reptilian head. "No. The Polongo River winds through the Rainy Basin, and this is the rainy season. Skybaxes can't fly well in the rain, and it's hard to see what's happening with the cloud cover. Somebody must go on foot."

Magnolia was aware that both Malik and Nallab were looking at her. She swallowed hard and glanced at Paddlefoot. She could tell that he was thinking the same thing she was. Who'd want to slog through the Rainy Basin in the rainy season? Not to mention that there was a good chance of meeting a Tyrannosaurus rex.

She tried to think about what Edwick and Calico would do. Yes, they would go. It was their duty. But they wouldn't rush off—they would make preparations.

"All right," the girl said calmly. "We need to plan things first. How long can the Spiral Clock be stopped before we have a serious problem?"

Malik answered, "I can keep track of things with my pocketwatch for about a week. But this is the middle of spring—there are plantings, hatchings, prunings. We can't go long without the clock."

She turned to Nallab. "You'll have to keep the citizens calm. Tell them that we'll solve this problem."

The old scholar nodded his head. "I understand. But I don't need to tell you—without the Polongo River, Waterfall City will die."

"I know," Magnolia said quietly. She thought for a moment before speaking again. "We've traveled all day, and it's almost dark. We'll start out at first light. We need supplies for a week and two Dimorphodons to relay messages. The people of this city are in a panic. You must tell them we are taking steps to solve the problem."

"I will do that now," said Nallab. The old man started out the door, then stopped. "How do you like your first day as Habitat Partners?"

Paddlefoot honked. "Never a dull moment."

Nallab chuckled. "We're glad you are here, believe me. I will send over some maps that may help you."

Paddlefoot and Magnolia stood on the observatory platform and gazed at the riverbed winding into the distance. After heavy rains, she'd seen the Polongo River swell over its banks, but she had never expected to see those banks empty. Magnolia had seen dry riverbeds in the desert, and they were always depressing, like a city without people and dinosaurs.

She could see dark clouds massing to the north of them. At least the Rainy Basin was living up to its name.

They studied the maps that Nallab had sent them, but they weren't much help. The water in the Polongo River was dropping, but they couldn't see where it could have gone. They finally decided that Malik was right. There was no way to know what was going on without journeying up the river.

Nallab walked out on the deck to join them, and he was carrying two Dimorphodons, one on each arm. "Here are your traveling companions," he told the Habitat Partners. "They are the best we have."

The Dimorphodons were small pterosaurs about the size of parrots. They were excellent at delivering messages. Some humans and dinosaurs considered them to be rather ugly and noisy, but Magnolia had always liked them.

"I grew up with Dimorphodons in the house," she

said. "My father is a message rider in Sauropolis."

Magnolia held out her arm to the small flyers. One of them immediately fluttered off Nallab's arm and landed on hers. She scratched the Dimorphodon under its chin and asked, "What's your name?"

"Bippa!" squawked the Dimorphodon. She snuggled against Magnolia's hand.

Seeing this, the other Dimorphodon flew to her arm, and she scratched under his chin, too.

"Peebo," he chirped.

"Bippa and Peebo," said the girl. "Are you good at remembering messages? This may be the most important message you'll ever carry."

Nallab waved his hand. "These two could memorize all the books in the library. They also know the countryside very well, and they're strong flyers."

Paddlefoot hooted. "I'll need a basket to carry them."

"We're packing your supplies now," said Nallab. "I think it's time you two had dinner and rested. You can't do more tonight, and you're leaving at first light. We've given you the guest quarters we use for champion Ring Riders."

"That wasn't necessary," said Magnolia. She was used to sleeping in barns and haylofts.

"Yes, it is," said Nallab. "You will see how grateful we are for what you're doing for us. Come."

Despite their worries about the river, the citizens of Waterfall City still managed to show Magnolia and

Paddlefoot their famous hospitality. Nallab showed them to a magnificent two-story cottage. The lower level had a ceiling twenty feet high and a bed of hay for Paddlefoot. The upper story had a lovely bedroom with a view of the entire city.

The Lambeosaurus snorted. "At least this job has some good points."

The best chefs served them dinner in the courtyard of the guest house. Magnolia ate delicious fruits, nuts, and honey bread, and Paddlefoot feasted on fresh, leafy vegetables. As promised, their supplies were already packed and ready to go. There was even a basket for the Dimorphodons, who were fast asleep inside of it.

Before going to bed, Magnolia gave the big Lambeosaurus a hug and an encouraging smile. "You aren't afraid of this quest, are you?"

"Yes!" he honked.

"Me too. But at least we have each other. Good night, partner."

The big dinosaur lowered his snout and tousled the hair on top of her head. It was his way of hugging.

Magnolia tried to sleep, but even on a soft bed, weary from a hard day, she found sleep difficult to come by. There was too much to think about, too much to worry about. What if they didn't solve the mystery of the lost river? What if Waterfall City became abandoned?

This was what she had wanted, she told herself, to

be a Habitat Partner. All her life she had wanted it, and she had begged her parents to allow her to apprentice. They weren't fond of the idea, because they had wanted Magnolia to follow in her mother's footsteps.

Her mother was a gardener who tended the famous Rose Gardens of Sauropolis, the capital of Dinotopia. That was an important job, to be sure, but Magnolia wanted to travel. There were Habitat Partners for the sky, forests, mountains, deserts, savannas, and beaches and bays. But she had chosen freshwater, because freshwater was everywhere on Dinotopia.

In her five years of apprenticeship, she had seen every lake, river, and swamp. She had visited every city, village, hatchery, and remote farmhouse. But she had never imagined the day when all the freshwater flowing to those places would be her responsibility. That day had seemed too far off to think about. Now it was here, and she was frightened.

Suddenly, the words of Tok Timbu came to her mind: "It is the master's decision to say when the apprentice is ready."

Edwick had decided that she was ready. She'd never questioned the decisions of Edwick and Calico before, so she shouldn't question their final decision. She should do the best she could, and bear the banner of the water lily proudly.

With that comforting thought, Magnolia was finally able to lose herself in sleep.

CHAPTER 4

At first light, Magnolia rousted herself from bed. She washed her face, brushed her teeth, and put on her new uniform. Gosh, it looked great, she thought. She wished she was going to march in a parade instead of going to trudge through the wilderness. The uniform would be ruined by nightfall.

She opened her door and found her breakfast waiting for her on a tray. She tried to enjoy the meal of fruits, nuts, and grain, knowing it would probably be her last civilized meal for a while. Then she went down the stairs of the guest house and found Paddlefoot enjoying his breakfast.

Two stableboys offered to help her load the supplies and the Dimorphodons on top of Paddlefoot, but she did it herself. The Lambeosaurus was very particular about how things were packed on his back. The Dimorphodons didn't like being awake so early, and they squawked in protest when she picked up their basket.

"Sorry, Bippa and Peebo," Magnolia said to them

in soothing tones. "The sooner we leave, the sooner we'll be back." That seemed to calm the little pterosaurs, and she made sure they had a good breakfast too.

Dawn was breaking over Waterfall City, casting a golden glow on the magnificent buildings. But the river had fallen more overnight, and the mists that always hovered over the city were gone. Magnolia couldn't ignore the dried fountains and canals, the still waterwheels, the boats mired in the mud, and the ominous quiet. Without water, the city was like an empty sea shell—pretty but useless.

Magnolia remembered what Master Edwick had told her as he lay injured in bed: "Freshwater is the lifeblood of Dinotopia." For the citizens of Waterfall City, water was more than blood; it was everything. These thoughts made her anxious to get moving.

When they reached the main street of Waterfall City, Magnolia was very surprised to find hundreds of people and dinosaurs waiting to bid them good-bye. It was not a joyous send-off; there was no clapping and cheering. The serious faces reflected the gravity of their mission.

She and Paddlefoot nodded somberly to the citizens as they walked down the street. Malik and Nallab were waiting for them at the rear gate of the city, which overlooked the barren riverbed.

"Your bravery will always be remembered," said Nallab.

"I hope it's our success that will be remembered," answered Magnolia.

"Be careful," warned Malik, "and return to us. We can't afford to be without you or the river."

The sad faces were too much to bear, and Magnolia was relieved when they finally left the city behind them. She turned her attention away from the gleaming buildings to the lush rain forest ahead of them. Black thunderclouds were already massing over the green hills. It was an unusually gray day for Dinotopia.

For most of the morning, the partners followed a path that ran alongside the barren riverbed. Soon, however, the underbrush and plant growth grew too thick for even Paddlefoot to walk through it. The path disappeared, and the big dinosaur finally had to stop.

"I guess nobody walks along the river into the Rainy Basin," said Magnolia. "What do you want to do?"

Paddlefoot shrugged his huge shoulders. "I guess we could walk down there, in the riverbed."

"I guess so," agreed Magnolia. Although the riverbed was as wide as always, the water flowed in several streams with dry sand between them.

She held on tightly as the Lambeosaurus slid down the bank into the riverbed. With most of the water gone, they could see rocks, fallen logs, and water plants that were withering in the air and sunlight.

There were also a number of dead fish.

A dying river is not a pretty sight, thought Magnolia. If they didn't save the river, it would be a scar upon the land for years to come.

The Lambeosaurus snorted loudly. "Smells bad down here," he said.

"Get used to it," Magnolia answered. "We may have a long way to travel in this riverbed."

"Not much to eat down here either," grumbled the dinosaur.

Magnolia laughed. To fuel his huge body, Paddlefoot had to spend almost half his waking hours eating. It helped that he could eat, and did eat, almost everything that grew in Dinotopia.

"Anytime you're hungry," she said, "feel free to go up to the bank and get a snack."

That made him feel better, and Paddlefoot began to walk swiftly along the riverbed. Magnolia kept looking at the rocks and sand, hoping to find a clue about what had happened to the river. But there weren't any clues—only miles of rocks, sand, dead fish, and dying plants.

About midday, the gray clouds rolled overhead and dumped sheets of rain on them. Paddlefoot didn't care about getting wet, but the Dimorphodons squawked like crazy. Magnolia picked up the pterosaurs and cradled them in her lap, trying to keep them dry. It didn't help that she was soaking wet herself. But there was no time to stop and seek

34

shelter—they had to keep moving.

The Lambeosaurus stopped a few times to eat, using his height to grab leaves off trees that grew along the bank. He often munched mouthfuls of leaves as he walked. The rain finally stopped, but the clouds didn't go away. It seemed as if the sun would never shine again.

Don't get depressed, Magnolia told herself. This is only the first day. But it felt as if they would have to walk all the way to the headwaters of the Polongo to find out what had happened. And what if it was still a mystery when they got there?

Again, she reminded herself that she had wanted this job. If they had been following Edwick and Calico, instead of going by themselves, she probably wouldn't have been worried at all. But Edwick and Calico were a long way away, and they couldn't help. She and Paddlefoot had to do this job alone, and that was even more frightening to her than the missing river.

Paddlefoot could sense her sadness and fear, and he began to sing. Well, it wasn't really singing—it sounded more like French horn playing. He made low mournful hoots that almost formed a melody. Some dinosaurs were beautiful singers, but he wasn't one of them.

The Dimorphodons took up the song too. They were even worse singers, with voices like screeching wheels that needed oil. Magnolia laughed at the terrible music and finally joined in. She couldn't make it sound any worse. Besides, singing was making the time go faster.

They were so busy screeching, honking, and hooting that no one was paying any attention to the river bottom. No one noticed that the sand was getting softer and softer, not even Paddlefoot. Without warning, the big dinosaur sank up to his hips in quicksand!

Magnolia screamed as he went down. The Dimorphodons flew off, screeching, into the trees. Paddlefoot trumpeted in terror and tried to get out. But the more he struggled, the deeper he sank into the treacherous quicksand. Magnolia could barely hang on.

"Stop! Stop!" she cried. "That's not working! You're just getting us *deeper!*"

"I know!" wailed the Lambeosaurus. He was now up to his thick waist in the soggy sand.

"Just stay calm," ordered Magnolia, trying to sound calm herself. She looked around and saw that the pool of quicksand was too wide for her to jump over and get help. She could send the Dimorphodons for help, but they were nowhere to be seen. Not only that, but she hated to have to send for help after only half a day of travel.

The girl tried to remember everything that Edwick had told her about quicksand. It really was mostly water with sand mixed in. True, you could drown in water, but you could also *float* in water! And floating in water would allow you to get your legs free. With your legs free, you could swim! Sort of.

"We can float in this stuff," she told Paddlefoot. "See if you can spread out on your stomach."

"But that will just make us go deeper!" moaned the dinosaur.

"No, it won't. Struggling will make us go deeper, but floating will keep us on top. Try it. What have you got to lose?"

The dinosaur honked fearfully and tried to stretch out on top of the pool of quicksand. When he began to sink up to his neck, he shrieked with panic. Magnolia almost fell off again.

"No," she said calmly, "don't struggle. I know that you like to use brute strength, but that won't work here. Just stay calm, spread your legs out, and float. Pretend you're in Deep Lake on a lazy afternoon."

Paddlefoot nodded, although he still looked frightened. But he did as he was told and stretched out on his massive limbs. Although it felt as if they were sinking deeper, they really weren't. They floated on the quicksand like a boat stuck in the reeds.

"My legs," said Paddlefoot with amazement, "they're free! A little bit anyway."

Floating was possible, but it didn't look as if swimming would be possible. Every time the big dinosaur moved his legs, they sank deeper. Magnolia had a feeling that if she jumped off, she might be able to swim out of the quicksand alone. But she didn't want to leave her friend.

So they just floated in the quicksand, a big lump, unable to move.

"Where are those stupid Dimorphodons?" she muttered.

"They're not so stupid." Paddlefoot snorted. "They're not stuck in the quicksand, are they?"

At this point, Magnolia didn't even care that she would be embarrassed to send the Dimorphodons back to Waterfall City for help. She just wanted to get out!

Okay, now she had to tell herself to remain calm. They weren't going to drown—at least not for a while. They weren't sinking any deeper, even if they weren't getting out. She had some rope in her pack, and they had their brains. That's about all they had at the moment.

It was hard to say how long they sat mired in the quicksand, because every minute seemed like an hour. Then Magnolia began to have an even greater fear than her fear of drowning. They were at the edge of the Rainy Basin, and that was Tyrannosaurus rex territory! What if a meat eater came along and decided to make a meal out of them?

Would a meat eater be discouraged by quicksand? Not likely. They sort of lost their senses when they were hungry and saw food, especially food that couldn't run or fight back. A Tyrannosaurus might wade into the quicksand and attack them before he figured out it was dangerous.

Paddlefoot suddenly lifted his head and looked around. "What was that?" he asked nervously.

"What was what?" Magnolia had fairly good hearing, for a human, but she didn't hear anything.

"Something's coming!" hooted Paddlefoot. He began to struggle again, and they sunk deeper into the quicksand.

"Hold still!" shouted the girl. "Panic won't get us anywhere." But she felt like panicking herself.

"There!" hooted the Lambeosaurus, shaking his head toward the forest.

Magnolia followed his gaze into the overgrown forest with its towering trees and huge leafy plants. Like Paddlefoot, she heard it coming before she saw it—heavy footsteps, crunching through the underbrush.

It was the unmistakable sound of a large dinosaur headed their way!

CHAPTER 5

"Quiet," she whispered to Paddlefoot. "Maybe he won't hear us."

"Hear us?" honked the Lambeosaurus. "He's headed right toward us! And meat eaters can *smell* meat!"

So she wasn't the only one worried about meeting a Tyrannosaurus. Magnolia reached into her pack and pulled out her short knife. She looked at the pitiful utensil, which she used to slice fruit, wondering what good it would do against a full-grown Tyrannosaurus. It was barely as long as one of their teeth!

Now the crunching footsteps were so loud that it sounded like a pack of tyrannosaurs. She braced herself and held her breath, but she still jumped when the huge dinosaur burst through the trees.

It had three horns and a shield of armor around its face, and it walked on four legs, not two. Magnolia breathed a loud sigh of relief when she saw the Triceratops. Then she blinked with amazement when she saw a teenage boy sitting on its back. She blinked again when she saw her two Dimorphodons, perched on the boy's shoulders.

The lad was thin, with dark hair and ratty clothes, and he laughed out loud at them. "Well, look at this! All dressed up for a parade, and no place to go!"

"We're the Habitat Partners of Freshwater!" said Magnolia huffily.

"Right, and I'm the king of Dinotopia!" He laughed again.

Magnolia frowned and pointed to the water lily insignia on Paddlefoot's blanket. "See!"

"How do I know you didn't steal that blanket?" The boy sneered. "How old are you?"

"Thirteen."

"Hey, you can't fool me! I've seen the Habitat Partners of Freshwater. The human is an old man, and the dinosaur is a Saltasaurus. Besides, would the Habitat Partners of Freshwater allow themselves to get stuck in quicksand?"

"Yes!" Magnolia groaned. She frowned and tried to explain. "We've been the Habitat Partners for only two days. We were apprentices until Master Edwick got injured, and now we're on an urgent mission. Do you see why you have to help us get out?"

The lad looked thoughtful. "Well, you do have two smart Dimorphodons traveling with you. They searched us out as we were plowing our field and brought us here."

He frowned and shook his head. "I still can't believe you're only thirteen and already a Habitat Partner! I'm *fifteen*, and I can barely make it as a farmer. I tell you, life just isn't fair!"

Paddlefoot looked at the Triceratops and made a bunch of hooting sounds. Loosely translated, he asked, "Are you going to let these silly humans argue all day? Or are you going to help us get out?"

The Triceratops cocked its head. It was young but strong and full-grown. It made several grunting noises that Magnolia didn't understand.

The lad shrugged. "Rogo says we should pull you out. But he says you should have better sense than to walk in a riverbed. By the way, what happened to the river?"

Magnolia flapped her arms with frustration. "That's what we're trying to find out!"

The lad turned to the Dimorphodons and said. "We've got work to do. You guys had better find a place to watch."

At once, the tiny pterosaurs flew into the trees and perched on a branch. The young man jumped off the Triceratops and looked upriver. "Down there," he said, pointing. "There's a bunch of fallen logs washed up on the bank. We can use them as a ramp. Can you get them, Rogo?"

The mighty Triceratops went along the bank of the river, trampling the thick ferns and plants. Using the two long horns above his eyes and the shorter one on his snout, he pushed the logs around as if they were twigs. In a few minutes of work, he had pushed the logs to the edge of the pool of quicksand.

Now the lad began to help him move the logs into position. They stuck one end of each log deep into the quicksand, while leaving the other end on dry ground. As the boy had said, the logs formed a sort of ramp.

"Get your feet on them," he said to Paddlefoot. "They should give you enough traction to get out."

When the Lambeosaurus looked doubtful, Magnolia gently patted his neck. "Go ahead," she urged him. "Don't struggle—just walk out."

Paddlefoot took a deep breath and lowered his legs back into the quicksand. Magnolia could hear the logs cracking under his immense weight, but he was able to walk on them. With a mighty heave, he bounded out of the muck and stood panting on dry ground. Magnolia patted him proudly on the back.

In the trees, the Dimorphodons made happy chirping sounds.

Magnolia looked at the lad and nodded curtly. "Thank you."

He took off his ragged hat and bowed low. "Permit me to introduce your saviors. I'm Birch, and this is Rogo."

Magnolia rolled her eyes. Saviors, indeed! "I am Magnolia, and this is Paddlefoot. We appreciate your help, but we must be going now."

"Wait a minute," said Birch. "Where is it that you're going?"

She pointed. "Up the river, or what's left of it."

"So you didn't make that story up? You really are the Habitat Partners of Freshwater?"

"Yes!" she snapped. "I wouldn't lie about something like that. Now out of our way!"

"Wait a minute, Your Partnership," said Birch. "Would you like some company? We could go along with you—help you get out of quicksand, bogs, and such."

Magnolia bristled. "We don't need any help."

Birch smiled. "You sure needed help a moment ago. Besides, this is a free land. There's nothing to prevent us from walking along beside you."

Magnolia was about to tell him to mind his own business when Paddlefoot cleared his throat. "Let's not be hasty," he whispered. "Perhaps it would be wise to have some traveling companions."

"Are you serious?" sputtered Magnolia. "These two?"

Paddlefoot cocked his head. "I don't see any other two around."

Birch scrambled on top of the Triceratops and sat grinning at them. "So, are we on our way?"

Magnolia shrugged. "I suppose so. I think we can stay in the riverbed, but let's try to walk near the bank, away from the pools in the middle."

Birch clapped his hands, and the two Dimorphodons flew over and landed on the pair of horns above Rogo's eyes.

"Don't you forget," said Magnolia, "those Dimorphodons are assigned to *us*."

"Of course," said Birch with a smile. "But they *like* us."

Magnolia gave Paddlefoot a gentle slap on the neck, urging him forward. The big dinosaur snorted and took his place at the head of the strange convoy. As Magnolia had suggested, he stuck close to the bank, away from the mushy center of the river. Rogo, Birch, and the Dimorphodons filed in behind them, with the pterosaurs chirping cheerfully.

The girl shook her head, thinking that she had certainly had a run of lousy luck. First, Master Edwick got injured, forcing her and Paddlefoot to become the Habitat Partners. Then they arrived in Waterfall City just as the Polongo River disappeared. That forced them to embark on a dangerous quest through the Rainy Basin. Then they got stuck in quicksand had to be rescued, only to be stuck with their rescuers!

"So how do you get to be a Habitat Partner?" asked Birch cheerfully.

Magnolia made a sour face, knowing that Birch was behind her and couldn't see it. She wanted to ignore him, but she had been taught not to be rude. They had a trip of many miles ahead of them, so they might as well talk to each other, she decided.

She answered, "It happens differently with different Habitat Partners. Some of them have won a contest, like Ring Riding or the Sky Race. Others were tested for the job and selected from hundreds of dinosaurs and humans. For me, it was an old-fashioned apprenticeship."

Magnolia smiled in remembrance. "From the time I was little, real little, I wanted to be a Habitat Partner. I met Paddlefoot when he was pulling a flower cart for my mother, and we got along right away.

"We used to pretend we *were* Habitat Partners. We lived in Sauropolis, so we saw Edwick and Calico quite often. One day, my father presented us to them as apprentices. To everyone's surprise, they chose us, even though I was only eight years old."

She laughed. "We found out later that Edwick was famous for being hard on apprentices. He had taken on many of them, but none had worked out. He told us that teenagers were too headstrong, which is why he wanted a younger apprentice this time. We behaved ourselves and got along with them, but I didn't expect to become a Habitat Partner for many more years."

Birch shook his head. "Wow, you got lucky. We've had nothing but bad luck."

Magnolia wanted to say that she didn't consider herself lucky, but she held her tongue. Everybody had a story to tell—she might as well hear theirs.

"My parents were killed," the boy began, "when

their sky galley crashed. I was at home with my dinosaur nanny—I was only four years old. All my human family was gone, so I was raised by dinosaurs on a farm. That's why I can understand almost any dinosaur lingo, and I get along with them so well."

He chuckled. "I think of myself as half-dinosaur."

Then his voice grew somber. "I didn't want to leave the farm and all my dinosaur friends, but that's what you're supposed to do. When you reach a certain age, you're supposed to go out and start your own farm. So that's what me and Rogo have done."

He spit into the sand. "It's just that we're lousy farmers."

Magnolia shook her head in disbelief. "Why would you start a farm on the edge of the Rainy Basin?"

"Well," said Birch, "the land was available to anyone who wanted it. Plus, if you want to grow beans, you should be in a place where there is a lot of water."

He lowered his head. "We had too much water, and we were too far away from town. It took us forever to get our beans to market. Plus, we always had poor crops."

Magnolia shook her head. "You're fighting the jungle out here. It's not easy to move out native plants. Edwick always said that crops were like stepchildren, forced upon the soil. But the weeds and the things that grow naturally are the soil's real children."

"Yes, that's my story," grumbled Birch. "An orphan, a stepchild, always where I'm not supposed to be."

"I didn't mean it that way!" protested Magnolia. Suddenly she felt terrible. It was true—Birch had had a lot worse luck than she had ever had. Both her parents were alive, and she had been placed in a very successful apprenticeship. The rest of her life was laid out for her, providing she didn't fail this important mission.

"When we get back," promised Magnolia, "we'll find you and Rogo a good plot of land. When it comes to farming, finding the right land is half the battle."

"No," said Birch, shaking his head. "We've talked about this a lot. We want to do what you're doing—helping people. Hey, we helped you, and maybe we can help others!"

He patted the big Triceratops on his armor. "We're not cut out to be farmers, are we, Rogo? Besides, by the time we get back to our farm, the birds will have eaten everything. As far as I'm concerened, the jungle can have that lousy farm. Give us a life of adventure!"

Magnolia whirled around and angrily replied, "Do you think our life is constant adventure? It's days of riding in the rain, only to sit in a bog, measuring water levels. How about the days I spent sitting in a tree, counting water birds? That's *my* exciting and adventurous life!"

"You attend the big conferences," said Birch, "ride in parades, and make speeches."

Magnolia laughed. "Oh, I'm really looking forward to that, when notable dinosaurs like Bix and Brokehorn ask me questions for hours. Do you think I will get to keep this job if I don't do it right? No. This job is too important."

"I'll be happy to trade places with you," said Birch. "After all, you seem to think farming is easy. All you have to do is find the right land."

"I didn't say that," snapped Magnolia. "We've visited lots of farms, and we often help farmers with their irrigation ditches. I know that farming is tough. Maybe you just don't want to work hard enough."

"We worked plenty hard!" growled Birch. "We've worked from dawn to dusk, until our backs were creaking like old tree limbs. Plowing a field is a lot harder work than sitting in a tree, counting birds!"

Magnolia frowned. "Some of us could be a little more humble, a little more content with our lot in life."

"Hey!" yelled Birch, "that's easy for you to say. You got what you wanted, little Miss Habitat Partner. Just let me have one good break, one bit of luck, like you got. That's all I ask for."

The skinny lad snapped his fingers. "Wait a minute—you could make *us* your apprentices! Yeah, that's it. Now that you're the ones in charge, you need your own apprentices. And where could you find two better ones than us?"

"Under a rock," Magnolia whispered. Paddlefoot made a laughing sound.

"What did you say?" asked Birch suspiciously.

Rogo snorted and growled. He must have overheard her unkind remark, because Birch shouted, "Maybe next time we'll leave you in the quicksand!"

Magnolia was about to turn around and tell him to leave them alone right now when Paddlefoot suddenly stopped. It jarred the girl, and she found herself staring down at the ground.

"What's the matter?" she asked.

"If you weren't so busy arguing, you might have seen it," Paddlefoot grumbled. "Look down—at the tracks."

Magnolia quickly dismounted, and she felt the Triceratops and his young rider peering over her shoulder. The Dimorphodons grew very quiet, and there was no sound coming from anywhere in the dense forest.

She could clearly see several pairs of tracks in the wet sand. They looked like three-toed bird tracks, only much larger—these were made by tyrannosaurs. The tracks had to be recent, because this had been river bottom only yesterday.

"Wow," muttered Birch. "Tyros. They must be looking for water, huh, to come this far south?"

"Yes," said Magnolia. "We've got to get off the river."

CHAPTER 6

"Get off the river?" asked Birch. "Are you daft? Isn't that what you're looking for—the river?"

"Yes," answered Magnolia, glancing around the silent jungle. "And we're not finding it here, are we? This is where the river *was,* but it's not where the river is now. With quicksand and meat eaters in the riverbed, I'm in favor of traveling somewhere else."

"Oh," scoffed Birch, "don't worry about tyros. Rogo can defend us. Can't you, buddy?"

The Triceratops snorted and shook his center horn confidently. Magnolia smiled at the dinosaur and said, "I'm sure you'd put up a good fight, Rogo, but what if we're attacked by a pack of them? I didn't think I would have to worry about this so soon. Luckily, there is one place around here where tyrannosaurs won't go."

Birch frowned in thought. "They won't go into cities, because they don't like humans too much. Where else?"

She pointed into the jungle. "Hadro Swamp is just

to the west of us. It's too wet and doesn't have the kind of food they like, so they don't normally go there. Besides, I need to take water-level readings to see if the swamp has gained water lately."

"You're going to leave this almost-dry riverbed to walk in a swamp?" asked Birch in amazement. "You're going to a lot of trouble to get rid of us, aren't you?"

"If you want to go home," said Magnolia, "that's fine with me. The important thing is that we keep heading north. There's no water in the Polongo, so there must be a lot more water somewhere else. That's what we've got to find—the place where the water went. The river winds around, and we can check on it a dozen places farther north."

Birch shuddered. "I never go near Hadro Swamp. It's a nasty place."

Magnolia shrugged. "Go back to your farm, then, if you're afraid. At least Paddlefoot and I are familiar with the swamp. We don't know what could happen to us in this riverbed."

She gently patted Paddlefoot. "What do you think? Shall we try the swamp?"

The big Lambeosaurus hooted a few times and shifted around on his feet. He wasn't any more anxious to travel through the swamp than Birch was, but he realized the problems they faced. He finally answered her by bounding over the bank and trudging into the forest.

Magnolia glanced over her shoulder and saw the Triceratops and his rider hurrying after them. She smiled to herself, thinking that maybe Birch would realize that the life of a Habitat Partner wasn't all that easy.

Paddlefoot had to battle his way through the thick underbrush, while Rogo moved with ease. The Triceratops merely crushed or knocked down everything in his path. Paddlefoot finally stepped aside to let Rogo cut them a road through the jungle.

Magnolia was relieved when they found a narrow path that led northwest, but she checked to make sure there were no Tyrannosaurus tracks. She kept looking for evidence of the meat eaters, but she didn't find any. She hoped they were sticking to the riverbed, looking for water instead of food.

After several hours, the jungle gave way to the grassy marshlands of Hadro Swamp. As far as Magnolia could see, there was nothing but tall clumps of grass surrounded by slimy brown water. A few scraggly trees popped up here and there, and a flock of birds dotted the air. The ripe smell of rotting plants was strong.

Like every human, Magnolia preferred clear streams and deep lakes to swamps. But she knew Hadro Swamp was an important part of the ecosystem. It captured water during the rainy season and held it for use during the dry season. Rivers were wonderful, but river water was escaping to the sea. The swamp collected water for all of Dinotopia to use.

"Yuck!" said Birch as he and Rogo came to a stop beside them. "What good is all of this?"

"You could stand to learn a few things," said Magnolia. "During the dry season, this water runs off into rivers, streams, and irrigation ditches. A lot of this water returns to the sky to become rain again. Without this swamp, Dinotopia might be a desert."

"Okay," said Birch, "but nothing can live here."

"Wrong again," answered Magnolia. "There's a whole world living in these shallow waters. You've got birds, turtles, snakes, frogs, fish, and several kinds of water dinosaurs."

Birch grumbled. "It sounds as if you *like* it here."

Magnolia pointed down. Nestled under some overhanging reeds was a beautiful water lily, floating on its lily pad. She pointed to the matching water lily on Paddlefoot's blanket.

"To the Habitat Partner, there is no body of water on Dinotopia more important than Hadro Swamp," she declared.

A smile crept across Birch's face. "Hey, at least there's food here." He tapped Rogo and pointed at a gnarled tree. "Head over there."

Magnolia's attention was drawn back to the water, where she saw a stream of bubbles popping to the surface. Some large creature was just under the surface, watching them. When she looked up, she saw Birch pick a large yellow fruit off the tree and put it to his mouth.

"Stop!" she yelled. "That's poisonous!"

Birch looked at her in amazement. "This is poisonous? It looks delicious."

"It's a swamp apple," explained Magnolia, "not a real apple. Actually, there is one month out of the year when swamp apples are safe to eat."

"Is this the month?" asked Birch.

Magnolia smiled. "I don't know. Why don't you find out?"

"You know everything else," scoffed Birch.

Magnolia sighed. "Edwick told me that you can eat swamp apples when they're very ripe. But he said he would never eat one unless he saw it fall off the tree in front of him."

Birch frowned at the apple and finally threw it into the water. At once, a mass of silvery fish swirled around the fruit, eagerly tearing it apart.

"The fish don't think it's poisonous," he said.

"Are you a fish?" asked Magnolia. She stared past him. "There is something interesting about that tree, though."

"Oh, yeah. What?"

She pointed to the base of the tree trunk, where there was a ring of dried mud. "That's a high-water mark, probably several weeks old. It doesn't look as if the water in the swamp has been rising. The level is about where it should be, maybe even down a little."

"So the river didn't empty into the swamp," said Birch. "Does that mean we can get out of here and back to dry land?"

"Not so fast," said Magnolia. She peered at the sun, which was low in the western sky. "It's going to be night in an hour or two, and I still have to take measurements. I think we should find a place to spend the night."

Birch's jaw dropped open. "We're going to spend the night in a *swamp*?"

"Not in the water. There are small islands throughout the swamp—I'm sure we can find one." She said a few words of encouragement to Paddlefoot, and the hadrosaur splashed into the water.

"Don't you think we should take a vote or something?" asked the lad.

"It's a free land," answered Magnolia, throwing his own words back at him. "You didn't have to come with us. You wanted to, remember?"

Paddlefoot headed north, half-swimming and half-walking in the brackish water. Magnolia turned around to see Birch and Rogo, who were having a much more difficult time of it. The big Triceratops had smashed his way through the forest with ease, but his stubby legs and squat body weren't meant for swamp travel. It was all Rogo could do to keep his nose above the water.

It didn't take long for the Dimorphodons to figure out that they were on the wrong dinosaur. They fluttered off Rogo's horns and returned to their basket on Paddlefoot's back. As Rogo struggled through the water, Birch got soaking wet. But he didn't complain.

"Better slow down," Magnolia whispered to Paddlefoot. The Lambeosaurus nodded and slowed his pace to an easy swim, letting Rogo and Birch catch up.

It never ceased to amaze Magnolia how some creatures were perfectly suited to one terrain, and no good in another. Some, like Paddlefoot, could swim fairly well. Others, like Rogo, could cut a path through a forest. Still others could race like the wind over the plains, or soar through the sky.

So it was with people, Magnolia decided. Not all of them had the same talents, the same abilities. Some were amazing gardeners, like her mother, and some were wonderful teachers, like Nallab. And a few were good at lots of different things, but not great at any one thing.

Magnolia knew she had been a good apprentice, and she hoped she would be a good Habitat Partner. If she failed at it, she didn't know what she would do with her life. She didn't want to think about it.

The girl glanced back at Birch, who looked wet and miserable sitting atop the struggling Triceratops. Even though he was a cocky fifteen-year-old, she began to feel sorry for him. It must be terrible, she thought, not to know what to do with your life. Even though Birch had been raised on a farm, he had failed as a farmer. What was he going to do now?

She *was* lucky, Magnolia decided. She would never consider herself unlucky again.

Gradually, Magnolia became aware of long shadows stretching across the swamp. A cold breeze came off the dark water, bending the tall grasses and reeds. The girl shivered. Night was coming, but they weren't making very good time because of Rogo. Unfortunately, they hadn't seen anything that looked like an island.

Even though Paddlefoot was at home in the water, Magnolia didn't want to slog through a swamp in the dark. Rogo and Birch would never make it.

"Let's rest a moment," she said to Paddlefoot. She held up her hand to stop Rogo and Birch, too.

The poor Triceratops stumbled around, trying to find a sandbar to stand on. Birch pulled his sopping wet legs out of the water with a moan.

"Hey," he said. "We're ready to hit that island anytime now."

Magnolia shrugged apologetically. "I'm sorry, but I haven't seen one. And it's getting dark."

"No kidding," muttered Birch. "And I wouldn't mind seeing a swamp apple fall off a tree about now, because I'm getting hungry."

"That's no problem," said Magnolia. "I've got enough food for us, although it will only last half as long if the both of us are eating it."

Something caught her eye in the dark water—

more of those little bubbles. Whatever was making them was waiting and watching, just under the surface.

"Can you really talk to any dinosaur?" she asked.

"Try me," answered Birch.

She pointed into the black water. "Will you dive in right there?"

"Are you crazy?" asked Birch.

"No. You're soaking wet anyway, so what's the difference? We need to ask directions, and there's somebody who might help us under the water. Somebody who's been following us since we got here."

"Uh," said Birch worriedly, "what if this somebody's a meat eater?"

"It probably is," said Magnolia, "but mostly a fish eater. You haven't become a fish yet, have you?"

"In this place," grumbled Birch, "I wish I was a fish." The boy said something to Rogo, and the Triceratops nodded somberly.

"What did you tell him?" asked Magnolia.

"I told him that if I start screaming for help, he should help me. And so should you."

"You worry too much," said Magnolia.

Birch stood on Rogo's back and swallowed a big gulp of air. Then he plunged into the brackish water. Magnolia found herself getting tense, and she wondered if she had made a terrible mistake. It seemed like a long time before anybody came up.

Finally, both of them shot to the surface. The boy

looked small next to the huge creature that floated in front of him. With its long tail, the scaly reptile looked like a log—with teeth.

Out of all the creatures on Dinotopia, Rutiodon was the only one who had relatives all over the world: crocodiles, alligators, and caimans.

The mouth of the giant Rutiodon gaped open, and Magnolia thought that it would swallow Birch in one bite. Instead, the dinosaur made several grunting sounds. The boy grunted back. They conversed like this for several moments, until the Rutiodon rolled onto its back and pointed its tail toward the setting sun.

"There's an island due west of here," Birch translated. "Pogwog says if we hurry, she thinks we can make it before dark."

"The Habitat Partners thank you," said Magnolia to the Rutiodon.

Both Paddlefoot and Rogo made their own peculiar sounds of thanks. Pogwog swished her tail and vanished under the water. Then Birch swam over to Rogo and climbed aboard.

"I'm impressed," admitted Magnolia. "You really *can* talk to dinosaurs. We'd better get going."

With Paddlefoot in the lead, they splashed through the swamp toward the setting sun.

It was nearly dark before Paddlefoot lumbered ashore onto the small spit of land. It was so covered with reeds and grass that they never would have found it if they hadn't known it was there. Magnolia patted her partner on the neck and leaped down. Her legs were stiff and painful from the long hours of riding.

Rogo was so glad to get his feet back on dry land that he whimpered as he came ashore. As soon as Birch got off, the big Triceratops lay upon the ground and panted with exhaustion. Life in the swamp was definitely not for a Triceratops.

She took the Dimorphodons' basket, the supplies, and the blanket off Paddlefoot's back. At once, the Lambeosaurus waded back into the water and began to chomp on a stunted tree. After a few moments, the tree was gone, branches and all.

"That doesn't look like a bad idea," said Birch with a smile. "You said you had some food?"

"Yes," answered Magnolia, opening the saddlebag. "Let's see what they gave me. How about a loaf of bread?"

"Sounds great!" exclaimed Birch. He snatched the loaf out of her hands.

"Not the whole loaf!" she cautioned. "This food has to last for several days."

"Oh, right," said the lad. He tore off a large chunk and handed the rest back to her. He ate nearly as fast as Paddlefoot, and the bread was gone in a few seconds. Then he stretched out on the ground beside his friend, Rogo. The two of them were asleep, and snoring, within seconds.

Magnolia fed some of her bread to the Dimor-phodons and looked up at the sky. Between the gray clouds, she could see a handful of stars and a sliver of moon. It seemed strange to be out here in the wilds without Edwick and Calico. She could remember hundreds of nights she and Paddlefoot had slept in places like this, but never without Edwick and Calico.

When Paddlefoot got back from eating his dinner, he looked puzzledly at their snoring companions. "What happened to them?"

Magnolia smiled. "I guess the life of a Habitat Partner isn't as easy as they thought it would be."

"No," hooted the dinosaur. "But how would we look after plowing a field all day?"

"That's true," admitted Magnolia. "Do you think we'll find the river tomorrow?"

Paddlefoot shook his head. "Who knows? We can only do our best."

"Yes," agreed Magnolia. "We can only do our best. Good night, my friend."

"Good night," honked the Lambeosaurus. The island wasn't big enough for Paddlefoot to lie down, so he closed his eyes and went to sleep right where he stood.

Magnolia stretched out on the ground and pulled a handful of reeds around her for warmth. She looked up at the cloudy sky and hoped it wouldn't rain.

CHAPTER 7

At first, Magnolia thought it *was* rain that woke her up, because something was tapping on her face. She brushed her hand across her face to get the water off, but there was no water. She bolted upright on her bed of reeds and felt things moving in her hair. A second later, they were crawling all over her body!

She jumped up and began swatting at them, but the large insects kept buzzing all around her. Dawn was just creeping over the mountain to the east, and she could plainly see her attackers. The little island was engulfed in a swarm of dragonflies!

"What the heck is this?" shouted Birch, leaping to his feet.

"Dragonflies!" answered Magnolia. The dinosaurs, with their thick skin, were hardly bothered. They kept right on sleeping. The Dimorphodons were flying at the swarm, gorging themselves on the four-winged insects. Dragonflies were one of their favorite foods.

The insects swirled around the two humans, attracted by the scent and moisture on their skin. Birch looked like a man possessed as he leaped around, swatting and shouting.

"You didn't tell me about this!" he yelled.

"I told you lots of things lived in the swamp. I forgot to mention the insects!"

"What'll we do?"

"Get out of here!" She pounded on the rib cage of the big Lambeosaurus. "Paddlefoot, wake up!"

"Huh?" snorted the dinosaur drowsily.

"Wake up!" Magnolia shouted again. "We're being attacked by a swarm of dragonflies!"

Birch couldn't stand it anymore, and he leaped off the island into the water. Magnolia struggled to throw Paddlefoot's blanket onto his back, followed by the supplies and the basket. The trouble was that she could barely see in the dim light and the swarming insects. Then she had to put the Dimorphodons in the basket when they plopped to the ground, unable to fly because they'd eaten so many dragonflies.

Rogo continued to sleep, snoring loudly. Paddlefoot sounded a piercing note through his crest, and the Triceratops staggered to his feet. He shook his horns, ready to do battle, but the insects just swirled around him. His mighty horns were of no use against these creatures.

"Rogo!" shouted Birch from the water. "Let's get out of here!"

The Triceratops stumbled into the swamp. Birch clung to his back, but he didn't climb aboard. He didn't want to leave the safety of the water.

"Head north!" shouted Magnolia, pointing in that direction. She ran her fingers through her hair, tossing the bugs out. Then she pulled her hat tight over her head to keep them out.

Paddlefoot dropped to his knees, and the girl scrambled aboard. She held on for dear life as the Lambeosaurus jumped off the island and landed in the water with a huge splash. The wake from the splash swirled around them as they struggled forward. For once, Rogo and Birch were moving faster, and they were already in the lead.

The swarm of dragonflies was enormous—it seemed to blacken the sky. Magnolia finally just rested her head on Paddlefoot's broad back and covered her face against the tiny tormentors. She would have to count on her partner to get them away from this bizarre attack.

Magnolia tried hard not to blame the insects, who were only looking for food. It had been blind chance that the swarm had stumbled upon their little sleeping place. Still, it made her realize why so many of the creatures of the swamp lived under water.

Finally, she couldn't feel the insects striking her skin, and she looked up to find that the swarm was behind them. Rogo and Birch were still ahead of them, but they were slowing down. Birch climbed onto the back of the Triceratops and waved at her.

The sun painted a golden streak across the vast expanse of water. Even the swaying reeds looked golden green. It was morning on the marsh.

"Nice way to wake up!" called Birch. "I know you're fond of the swamp, but I'm ready to get out of here!"

"Soon!" promised Magnolia. She could see the small mountain to the east of them and a larger mountain range to the north. She had a good idea where they were, and she wanted to travel father north before they cut back to the river.

"I still have to take some measurements," she said. "If you find a good place to stop, we can have some breakfast too!"

As expected, that suggestion hurried Rogo and Birch along. On their own, they located another tiny spit of land and dragged themselves ashore. Once Paddlefoot waddled ashore, there was hardly enough room for all of them to stand. The Dimorphodons flew down to their roost in the basket, and it was a full crew.

As the dinosaurs munched whatever greenery they could find, Magnolia and Birch finished off the rest of the loaf of bread. Everyone felt better after having breakfast and drying off.

As Birch watched with curiosity, Magnolia took a weighted length of rope from her saddlebag. She dropped the weight into the water and counted off the markings on the rope.

"You look sad," Birch remarked.

"Do I?" asked Magnolia. "My master, Edwick, was doing this same thing when he was injured. It reminded me of him, that's all. I hope he's all right."

"If he's in a nice soft bed," said Birch, "he's doing better than we are. Don't we need to head back to the river now?"

"If you look to the east of us, there's a small mountain. The Polongo goes around that mountain and then curls back. If we go farther north, we'll actually have a shorter walk to the river."

Birch nodded. "Okay. I guess you know what you're doing."

The girl sighed. "I hope so." She began to pull in the rope.

"What did you find out?"

"Not much," Magnolia admitted. "As I expected, the water level in the swamp is normal. The Polongo River isn't emptying into here."

"So our job just got harder, right?"

"Yes," said Magnolia, staring into the distance. "This means the river got diverted even farther north. We may have to go all the way to the headwaters to find the problem."

"Have you ever been there?" asked Birch.

"Just once. It's a mountainous area, hard to get to. You know, you and Rogo don't have to come along with us. I wouldn't blame you at all if you turned back and went home. This is our responsibility, not yours."

The skinny young man smiled and brushed the bangs off his forehead. "Hey, for you it may be normal to get attacked by dragonflies, but it never happened to me before! I want to see things I never saw, have things happen to me that never happened to me! I want to travel all over Dinotopia."

Magnolia crouched down by the water and washed off her measuring rope. "You could travel without being in this much danger and hardship. Why don't you take the regular roads, or a sky galley?"

The boy frowned. "My parents were killed in a sky galley, remember."

"I'm sorry," said Magnolia with a frown.

Birch shrugged. "I told myself that I didn't want to travel, because they got killed while they were traveling. But I always knew that was wrong—staying at home and farming is not for me. Rogo feels the same way I do. We want a job like yours!"

"After a few more days of this," said Magnolia, "you may feel differently." She turned to look back at the dinosaurs. "Everybody get enough to eat?"

"Not really," hooted Paddlefoot. "I don't think there's enough to eat in this whole swamp."

Birch laughed at the joke, and Magnolia looked at him. He really did have an amazing talent for understanding dinosaurs.

"Let's go," she said. "Due north."

The humans mounted the dinosaurs, and the Dimorphodons flew back into their basket. Once again, Rogo and Paddlefoot plunged into the brackish water and began paddling toward the north, where there was a lost river waiting to be found.

Black clouds swirled overhead, and Magnolia eyed them suspiciously. High in the clouds, she could see flashes of lightning, like blasts of sunlight that blinked for a moment, then went out. She hoped the lightning didn't come any lower. The last thing she wanted was for her tiny party to be stuck in a swamp during a thunderstorm.

She and Paddlefoot had taken the lead again, and she whispered to the Lambeosaurus. "I think we'd better get back to dry land."

Paddlefoot nodded in agreement, and he began swimming east. Magnolia waved to Rogo and Birch.

"Time to head east!" she called.

"No kidding!" said Birch, looking up at the angry sky. His words were punctuated by a loud rumble of thunder. The boy said something to Rogo, and the Triceratops quickly changed course.

Magnolia could see thick tendrils of rain in the distance. They reached down from the clouds and played across the mountaintops. A streak of lightning etched a blazing path through the black sky and struck the mountain. A few seconds later, she jumped as a crack of thunder jolted her senses.

The Dimorphodons shrieked with fear, and Magnolia scooped them out of the basket and held them in her lap. The tiny pterosaurs stopped squawking, but they were still shivering. She didn't blame them— the sky looked darker now than it had during the night. Every few seconds, flashes of lightning gave the clouds an eerie brightness.

Birch called out, "What happens if we get hit by lightning while we're in the water?"

"You don't want to know," answered Magnolia.

The boy laughed nervously. "But lightning only strikes tall things, right? Like trees and mountains."

"Right," answered Magnolia. She didn't mention that there were no tall trees or mountains in this part of the swamp. If lightning hit the swamp, it was just as likely to hit them as anything else.

The rain stayed far away, on the mountains, but the lightning and thunder seemed to be getting closer. Lightning, without rain, was one of the most dangerous things on Earth, Edwick had always told her. Almost every forest fire in the history of Dinotopia had been caused by lightning.

"Hurry," she urged Paddlefoot. The big dinosaur's shoulders moved back and forth as he increased his paddling. She turned around to see that Rogo and Birch were falling farther behind. She wanted to tell them to hurry, but she knew that Rogo was going as fast as he could through the marsh.

"I see land!" Paddlefoot panted.

Just then, a bolt of lightning streaked through the dark clouds and blasted the jungle in front of the mountains. The roar of the thunder came only a few seconds later. Magnolia didn't need to tell Paddlefoot to hurry. The lightning was very close now.

The Dimorphodons began to squawk again, and Peebo fluttered his wings as if he wanted to take off. Magnolia held the pterosaurs tightly in her lap and cooed softly to calm them. She didn't want them flying around in this storm and getting hit by lightning. The success of her mission could depend upon the Dimorphodons. Plus, she liked the little flyers.

Suddenly, she was thrown back in her seat as Paddlefoot climbed out of the water and onto dry land. She gripped her reins to keep from falling off.

"Good job!" she told her partner. "Wait for Rogo and Birch."

The Lambeosaurus snorted and got down in a crouch, totally exhausted. Magnolia looked back and could see Rogo and Birch struggling toward them. The Triceratops' snout was barely above the water, and the boy had jumped off and was swimming alone.

"Come on!" she yelled in encouragement. "You can do it! Swim! Swim!"

A monstrous crack of thunder nearly deafened her, and the Dimorphodons wailed with fear. She gripped them tightly, knowing they would fly away. In their panic, their claws cut through the sleeves of her shirt and into the skin on her arms. She clenched her teeth to keep from crying out.

Finally, Rogo straggled ashore, huffing and puffing, and Birch wasn't far behind him. Both of them collapsed onto the grassy shore and just lay there, panting. Lightning flashed overhead, and thunder roared all around them, but there was no shelter.

At least, thought Magnolia, they would not be in the water if lightning struck.

Birch rolled over and looked at her. "On second thought," he rasped, "I don't want to be your apprentice. I don't ever want to see that swamp again as long as I live! If the Habitat Partners of Freshwater have to go into the swamp, forget it!"

Rogo snorted in agreement.

"Okay," Magnolia said with a smile. "I'll remember that."

Without warning, a huge streak of lightning came blasting out of the sky. It hit a palm tree just a few yards away, and the palm fronds at the top burst into flame! The dinosaurs and humans stared in horror as the palm tree turned into a giant fireball.

Magnolia's first instinct was to run, but the swamp at her back stopped her. There was nowhere to run. Besides she shouldn't run—she should *do* something! But what?

The fireball that had once been a palm tree was sending sparks flying all over the place. Gradually, nearby trees and bushes were catching fire. It seemed impossible with a storm going on, but a forest fire was starting before their eyes!

Magnolia looked up to the cloudy sky. There was rain in the mountains, but none where they needed it. She looked on helplessly as the fire began to burn out of control in the thick underbrush.

CHAPTER 8

Birch jumped to his feet and pointed at the burning palm tree. "Rogo! Knock it down!"

The Triceratops lowered his massive head and pawed the ground for a moment. Then he took off at a full gallop. The ground shook as he thundered toward the tree, and he struck it like a runaway wagon. There was a terrible cracking sound as the trunk snapped in two, then it slowly toppled to the ground.

Rogo finished the job by running to the fallen tree and tromping on its flaming leaves until the fire was out. His efforts kept the flames from spreading through the air, but several bushes and smaller trees were already on fire.

At once, Paddlefoot waded back into the swamp. He leveled his big tail and swung it at the water. Magnolia and Birch didn't even have time to get out of the way as a huge wave came off Paddlefoot's tail and doused the jungle.

Paddlefoot kept swinging his tail at the water until all of the flames were out. Thanks to the quick action of the dinosaurs, the fire had been put out before it could do much damage to the forest. Magnolia breathed a sigh of relief, and the Dimorphodons squawked happily.

Magnolia picked at her drenched clothes and smiled. "I always say, if you want to put out a fire, make sure you have dinosaurs with you."

Birch studied his own damp clothes and laughed. "Here we are, looking for a lost river, and we're *wet* all the time!"

Magnolia laughed so hard that tears rolled down her cheeks. It felt good to laugh. "If you're the Habitat Partners of the desert, you're in the desert," she said. "If you're the Habitat Partners of water, you're in the water!"

The teenagers laughed until they finally had to sit down on the ground. Paddlefoot and Rogo just looked at each other and shook their heads, as if to say, "Silly humans."

A few minutes later, the fun was over. The strange caravan was back to slogging their way through the jungle. They looked for a trail to the river but couldn't find one. Once again, Rogo took the lead and carved a trail where there wasn't one.

By midday, the rain, thunder, and lightning had disappeared, leaving only a few clouds in the sky. It left something else, too—a huge rainbow that stretched clear across the Rainy Basin. The rainbow cheered everyone up, and Magnolia began to think that maybe this would turn out to be a good day after all.

"Wouldn't it be great," she said, "if we got to the Polongo River and found that everything was back to normal?"

"Could that happen?" asked Birch doubtfully.

"Sure," answered the girl. "Maybe a bunch of fallen logs, a rockslide, or a mudslide dammed up the river. And maybe enough rain has fallen to wash whatever was blocking it away, so the river is back to normal."

Paddlefoot honked, as if he didn't believe it would be that easy.

"Well, you never know," said Magnolia defensively.

They never found a path, which didn't surprise the Habitat Partners. Very few people or dinosaurs traveled through the Rainy Basin. If they did, they traveled by armored caravan on the main road that went from Waterfall City to Treetown. A small party like this was unheard of, even with Rogo plowing a path for them.

It was late in the afternoon, and Magnolia knew they had to be getting close to the river. She listened for the sound of rushing water, but she didn't hear it. The girl kept telling herself that it was possible for the river to return to normal on its own. It *was* possible, but not probable.

She had hope until they climbed up a rise and saw

a huge gap in the trees ahead of them. There was no water in the gap. The dried riverbed still looked like an open wound across the land.

Magnolia's heart sank.

"Is that it?" asked Birch.

"I'm afraid so," answered the girl.

"It doesn't look as if it's changed any."

"It sure doesn't," she answered glumly. "Let's take a closer look."

The dinosaurs moved slowly down toward the river. There was no rush. When they got to the barren riverbed, Magnolia dismounted and climbed down the bank. There were still a few streams of water, but the mighty Polongo was no more.

In anger, she slapped her fist into her palm. Two days they had been traveling, and they had nothing to show for it! All they had found out was that the river hadn't emptied into Hadro Swamp. They were no closer to discovering the truth.

Magnolia felt like crying, but she knew that Birch and the dinosaurs were looking at her. They were waiting for her to lead them. She knew she had to be brave, so she put on a stern face and turned around to speak to them.

"We're in for a long walk now," she said. "If the river didn't flow into Hadro Swamp, it must have been diverted a lot farther north. We might have to go all the way to the headwaters. Rogo and Birch, this gives you another opportunity to leave us and return home. I would take it, if I were you."

Birch jumped down to look eye to eye with his big friend. They conversed in low murmurs that Magnolia couldn't understand. If they left now, she would be even sadder, but she would understand. This wasn't their responsibility. Nobody expected them to take part in this crazy quest.

"If you don't mind," said Birch slowly, "we'll stay with you. But can we stay out of the swamp?"

Magnolia smiled. "We've checked the only swamp around here, and the river didn't go there. From now on, we'll have to stick to the riverbed. But I don't know what to expect."

Birch shrugged. "Rogo and I haven't known what to expect all along."

"Well, now we'll be even," said Magnolia. "We have another hour or so of daylight, so let's get going. Remember to stick to the banks, away from the middle, where there might be quicksand."

Somberly, they walked along the dried riverbed, stepping among dead fish and dying plants. Both Magnolia and Paddlefoot kept a lookout for Tyrannosaurus tracks, but they didn't spot any. Nothing alive seemed to want to have anything to do with the river.

Then, in the distance, Magnolia spotted a strange object. It appeared to be something big and brown, lying in the middle of the riverbed.

"What's that?" Magnolia asked Paddlefoot.

"I don't know," the Lambeosaurus answered warily.

The girl motioned to Birch and Rogo. "Do you see that up there? Let's go slowly."

The boy nodded, and the Triceratops grunted. Cautiously, the tiny party made their way toward the object. No one said a word, and even the Dimorphodons were very quiet as they sat perched on Rogo's horns.

As they drew closer, Magnolia finally figured out what the object was—an overturned boat about twelve feet long. She could see where recent repairs had been made, but it was a nice boat, not made of reeds but of actual wood. A wooden boat was very unusual for Dinotopia, where trees were hardly ever cut down unless they were dead or diseased.

It wasn't hard to figure out what had happened. As the water level quickly dropped, the boat had become grounded. But boats don't sail themselves down a river, thought Magnolia. What had happened to the pilot? And the passengers, if any?

Paddlefoot sounded a hoot of warning, and Magnolia saw why. All around the boat were tracks—Tyrannosaurus tracks.

Magnolia surveyed the woods on both sides of the river, but no meat eaters jumped out to greet them. Of course, she told herself, the boat had lain here for three days now. Whoever was in it might be long gone, either walking or fallen prey to the meat eaters.

No one wanted to be eaten by a Tyrannosaurus, but that was considered a noble death on Dinotopia. It was a form of recycling to donate your flesh to the living. In fact, many dying Dinosaurs made a sacred journey to the Rainy Basin to feed the Tyrannosaurs. Others went to the Portal of the World Beneath, where the Pteranodons would feed upon them.

Still, at the young age of thirteen, Magnolia wasn't anxious to become somebody's dinner.

Birch asked, "Should we stop to look for whoever was in this boat?"

"I don't think we'll find them," said Magnolia. She glanced back at the meat eaters' tracks. "Let's keep moving."

"Hey! Hey!" called a distant voice. "Over here!"

The humans and dinosaurs all looked around to see where the voice was coming from.

"Over here! Over here!"

Paddlefoot, who had excellent vision, nodded his head toward a stand of tall palm trees. "That way."

The rest of them followed the Lambeosaurus as he made his way to the opposite bank. He stopped at the bank and craned his neck at the tallest tree. At the very top perched a white-bearded old man.

Magnolia looked curiously at him. "What are you doing up there?"

"What am I doing up here?" he shrieked. "Trying to keep from getting *eaten!* Do those dinosaurs eat people?"

"No!" scoffed the girl. "Really, very few dinosaurs are carnivorous. You can't tell the difference?"

"No," the old man sadly admitted. "When some other dinosaurs started chasing me, I climbed up here. They sure *acted* like they wanted to eat me."

"They probably did," said Birch. "They had big teeth, right? And little forearms."

"Yes," the man said with a nod.

"Good thing you climbed up there," Birch remarked. "Why don't you come down?" He patted the armor of his horned comrade. "Rogo will protect you."

"Really?" asked the bearded man. "I would like to come down. I'm tired of eating coconuts."

"Come on down," said Magnolia.

When the little man scuttled down the tree trunk, they saw that he was wearing strange clothes: a jacket with shiny gold buttons on it, and thick bell-bottomed pants.

"Are you a Dolphinback?" asked Birch.

"You mean, am I a newcomer to this strange land?" asked the man. "That I am! The name is Aaron Ruzzo!"

"Birch and Rogo," said the lad, pointing to himself and the Triceratops.

"Magnolia," said the girl, "and this is my friend Paddlefoot. We're the Habitat Partners of Freshwater. What exactly happened to you, if you don't mind our asking?"

"Well," Aaron Ruzzo began, "I, er, made a mistake, and the captain put me overboard in that lifeboat. I paddled through a fog and saw your island, but my boat crashed on the reef. I thought I was going to drown, until some dolphins grabbed me and pulled me to your fair shores."

He went on. "What was left of my lifeboat washed ashore after me. The people up north admired it so much that they repaired it. They said I should sail down the Polongo River to Waterfall City, where they would teach me all about Dinotopia. They helped carry my boat to the river."

Aaron shook his head. "You have strange rivers here. I'm drifting along with the current, and the river keeps getting shallower and shallower. Then I run aground! What kind of river is that, I ask you?"

"That's why we're here," said Magnolia. "We're trying to find out what happened to the river. Do you remember anything else that happened before the river went dry?"

Aaron stroked his beard. "Well, there was a big shaker—an earthquake! I remember the water splashing around and the trees swaying back and forth."

"Ah," said Magnolia thoughtfully. "I didn't know how far north the earthquake happened. That must be connected to the disappearance of the river."

"Can you take me to Waterfall City?" Aaron asked hopefully.

"Not right now," answered Magnolia. "We're going the opposite way, to find out where the water went. There's no point in going to Waterfall City now—everyone there is too frantic about the missing river."

"You'd better come with us," said Birch. "Unless you want to stay in that tree until we get back."

"What about my boat?" asked the little man with alarm. "I don't want to leave it!"

Magnolia shrugged. "I don't think you have much choice. When was the last time the meat eaters were here?"

"They came by this morning," answered Aaron. "Two of them. Just to make sure I was still up there."

"Let's get going!" said Magnolia, clapping her hands.

"Please," begged Aaron, "bring my boat! It's all I have in the whole world. You've got big dinosaurs there—can't they carry it?"

Birch shrugged. "That's their decision. If they want to bring it, they can bring it." He turned to Rogo, pointed to the boat, and made a few sounds.

The big Triceratops went to the lifeboat and sniffed it. Then he nudged it with his center horn. When it moved easily, he must have figured it was fairly light in weight. He turned to the old man and nodded.

Birch laughed. "I think Rogo is tired of swimming. There's no other reason why a dinosaur would ever want to carry a boat."

"It could be very useful," insisted the old man, "if we get some water back in this river."

Magnolia grabbed one side of the overturned boat. "Let's get it up on Rogo's back. We've got to get away from here, because the meat eaters will be back to check on Aaron."

That made the humans move quickly, and they lifted the boat onto Rogo's back. It was a perfect fit, although it did make the Triceratops look like a giant turtle with horns. Birch would have to walk now, but he didn't seem to mind. Aaron made sure to grab the boat's oars.

Magnolia pointed into the distance. "There's a bend in the river ahead of us. Let's get around it before the meat eaters come back."

Magnolia climbed onto Paddlefoot's back, and the group set off once again down the dry riverbed. Now they numbered seven—three humans, two big dinosaurs, and two little pterosaurs. Plus a boat.

Magnolia looked behind her at the strange procession and shook her head. If this oddball group managed to save the Polongo River, she would be amazed.

CHAPTER 9

That night, the black clouds returned and drenched them with rain. To Magnolia's surprise, the boat proved to be useful. She, Birch, Aaron, and the two Dimorphodons huddled under it to stay dry. Magnolia felt sorry for Paddlefoot and Rogo, who had no shelter. But they seemed unbothered as they stood guard and watched for meat eaters.

As the humans sat in the darkness under the boat, smelling the musty wood and listening to the rain, Magnolia and Birch asked Aaron about the outside world.

"You're not missing anything," grumbled the old man. "People lie and cheat, and they aren't always friendly to each other. I'm sorry to admit, I was one of the liars and cheaters. That's how I got into trouble— cheating at cards. Never cheat the captain of a ship at high sea."

He shook his head in amazement. "But here on Dinotopia, nobody seems to care what I did before. It's as if I've become a different person since coming here. Everybody I've met has been nice to me. Except, of course, for those toothy critters who tried to eat me. You people are right to keep this place a secret."

"It's nature that has kept it a secret," said Magnolia. "Without the help of the dolphins, no one could ever reach our shores. It's written that every person who arrives on Dinotopia is reborn."

"Yes," said Aaron somberly, "I believe that. Coming here forces you to throw out everything you know about people, and nature. I'm ready to chip in, but how am I supposed to repay you people for your kindness? What am I supposed to do with my life here?"

Birch muttered, "I'd like to know the answer to that question myself. I chose the wrong thing to do with my life."

"Me too, lad," said the old sailor. "Maybe you'll be given a second chance, like I was when the dolphins brought me here."

"I hope so," answered Birch. "Look at Magnolia— she's only thirteen years old, and she's got a very important job."

"That so?" asked Aaron. "This Habitat Partner business is important, huh?"

"Yes," said the girl glumly. "I only hope I can do it properly."

Aaron chuckled. "I was only thirteen years old when I first shipped out to sea. A cabin boy. I was scared to death. And seasick? My gosh, I was seasick for days! I thought they would just throw me over the side and be done with me."

He went on. "But the captain was a wise old buzzard. I wanted to stay below, but he ordered me to go up and sit on the deck and stay there. Day after day, night after night, I watched the rolling seas. Until I began to understand what was making the ship rock, and what was making me sick."

Aaron nodded his head. "One morning, I stood up and wasn't sick any longer. I finally had my sea legs. From then on, I was a crackerjack sailor, even if I did learn to enjoy gambling too much. Don't worry, missy, the same thing will happen to you. You'll wake up one morning and know this job belongs to you, and you belong to it."

Magnolia smiled. "I'm glad we met you, Aaron. Let's try to get some sleep, okay?"

"Sounds good to me," he said. "I can tell you, it's hard to sleep up in a tree, with hungry critters looking at you. Good night, all."

"Good night," they told the old sailor. Within a few seconds, he was snoring.

Magnolia shifted around under the boat and tried to get comfortable. She found herself leaning against Birch.

"Sorry," she said.

"That's okay," answered the young man. "You can lean against me. We'll keep warmer that way."

Her choice was to either lean against Birch, or lean against the rough wooden slats of the boat. It felt funny to be so close to a boy, in the dark, but it also felt sort of nice. The Dimorphodons cooed softly in her lap, and they didn't mind nestling. So she leaned into Birch and rested her head on his bony shoulder.

The rain was beating a gentle tattoo on the outside of the boat, and it lulled them to sleep.

The next morning, they crawled out from under the boat and greeted the new day. The sky was surprisingly clear and blue, and the air smelled as if it had been sweetened with perfume. Magnolia felt well rested, considering that she had slept under an overturned boat.

Paddlefoot was standing guard about a hundred feet to the south of them. Rogo stood guard to the north. She ran toward the big Lambeosaurus.

"Did you get some sleep?" she asked him.

"A little," he snorted. "The rain left after the moon rose high. We took turns staying awake to watch for signs of danger."

"That's good," said Magnolia. She turned to look north along the dry riverbed. "We have to try to make some distance today."

They ate quickly and loaded the boat onto Rogo's back. Nobody questioned the wisdom of bringing the boat with them anymore. Most of the way, Magnolia walked with Birch and Aaron, giving Paddlefoot a little relief. She didn't think the Lambeosaurus had really slept much the night before.

As they moved into the northern mountains, the terrain around them began to change. The lush growth of the jungle gave way to a pine forest, and they found themselves in a small canyon. It was nothing like the vast canyons around Canyon City, but it was a welcome change from the steamy jungle of the Rainy Basin.

One welcome result of moving to higher ground was that they were less likely to run into meat eaters. After a while, Aaron stopped looking over his shoulder, as if expecting a pack of tyrannosaurs to bear down on him.

Unfortunately, the higher terrain brought no change to the Polongo River itself. It remained as dead and barren as farther downstream. It fact, thought Magnolia, the sand on the river bottom even seemed a bit drier here. She was glad they didn't have to worry about quicksand, but she began to worry again about never finding the water.

Where had it gone?

There was nothing to do but stay calm, she told herself. She kept thinking about the old sailor's words of the night before. He said that one day she would get her "sea legs" and feel comfortable in her job as Habitat Partner. She began to wonder if that would ever happen.

More than likely, she would be a failure on her

first mission, and they would have to find somebody else to do it. Maybe they would even coax Edwick and Calico out of retirement.

As the afternoon wore on, the canyon began to narrow around them and grow higher. Magnolia had been up here only once before, several years ago, when Edwick had wanted to inspect the headwaters of the Polongo. That had been a rough journey, taking several days, because they had to walk around the river, not in it.

Normally, this canyon would be alive with the sound of rushing water and birds diving for fish in the river. Without the river it was silent, and the silence gave the canyon a spooky feeling, as if the travelers were walking into a tomb. The high canyon walls, striped with erosion, felt like the walls of a great cathedral.

Aaron felt it too. "I was just here a few days ago," said the old sailor with awe. "It was sure a lot different. A lot nicer."

"Water is the lifeblood," said Magnolia thoughtfully. "Without it, things die."

"I think it was along here that I felt the earthquake," said Aaron.

"Did the water level start to fall after that?"

"Yes," he answered. "Now that you mention it, I think it did! Of course, I had never been here before, so I didn't know what was happening until my boat ran aground."

Magnolia had her own vivid memory of the moment when the earthquake struck. She could still see Edwick crawling through the geyser as it spewed scalding water all over him. She could still see the burns on his face and arms, and his frail body lying in a bed.

It must have been a powerful earthquake, Magnolia decided, to be felt all the way west to Volcaneum and south to Waterfall City. It had probably been felt as far east as Treetown.

She could see the skies darkening overhead, but it wasn't more rain. It was nightfall again. Once the sun fell behind the mountains, the shadows deepened quickly in the canyon.

Another day, Magnolia thought sadly, without solving the mystery of the river. Another day of failure.

She was so depressed that she fell back and let Paddlefoot take the lead. For a mile or two, she did nothing but stare at the ground and kick stones. She didn't see the Lambeosaurus as he rounded a bend in the river far ahead. But she heard him loud and clear when he trumpeted a sound of alarm.

"What was *that?*" shouted Aaron.

"That was Paddlefoot," answered Magnolia, running forward. "Let's see what he's found!"

Magnolia ran forward with Aaron and Birch beside her. Rogo, who had been guarding the rear, thundered past them, with the boat bouncing on his back.

It didn't matter who got to Paddlefoot first, because it was perfectly clear why he had trumpeted.

In front of them, blocking the river, was a giant pile of rocks and boulders. Some of the boulders were as big as a house! Magnolia looked up at the canyon wall on the eastern side and saw a huge V-shaped gap where the avalanche had occurred. It was a massive one, the biggest avalanche she had ever seen.

Still, she thought, there ought to be water washing over this accidental dam. But where was the water? Only Paddlefoot was tall enough to see over the giant wall of rocks.

"Paddlefoot, can you see what happened to the water?" she asked.

The Lambeosaurus stood on his hind toes and stretched his neck. He needed every inch of his twenty-foot height to look over the dam.

"The water is there!" he hooted. "But it's flowing into a hole in the canyon!"

"Let me see!" shouted Magnolia. She ran up the dinosaur's tail and across his back until she reached the top of his head. She hung on to his crest as she peered over the jagged wall of rocks.

Not only had the earthquake caused an avalanche—it had opened a chasm in the rock wall! With its natural path blocked, the river was flowing into this new canyon. There was no way to tell where it was going, but the frothy water that belonged in the

Polongo River was coursing with its usual strength and purpose.

"What's happening?" called Birch.

"There's a chasm in the canyon wall!" Magnolia shouted back. "We have a new river, but I can't tell where the water is going!"

Birch asked, "If we can move these rocks—somehow—will that get the water back on track?"

"No!" answered Magnolia. "That won't be enough. We've got to plug up this hole too!"

"That's going to be a big job," said Paddlefoot.

Magnolia gazed with concern at the darkening sky. "We know only half the story. To make the proper decisions, we have to know where the new river is going. Maybe it flows just a short distance, and we can easily divert it back to its regular path. Aaron, may I borrow your boat?"

The old sailor scratched his head. "I guess so. But, missy, that's some angry-looking water."

"Do you plan to go right now?" asked Birch with alarm.

"Yes," answered Magnolia. "Every minute is important."

"Then I'll go with you," said Birch.

"Me too," said Aaron. "You'll need an old salt to help you with that boat."

Magnolia shook her head firmly. "I can't let either of you go. This is *my* job."

"Don't be a fool, missy," said the old man. "You'll need two people to row, while you can keep the lookout. You're the one who knows what to look for. It's the only way, especially if we have to row against the current."

The girl sighed. They were right, of course. She didn't know what to expect, and she was hardly able to row the boat by herself. On Dinotopia, people always helped one another, even if there was danger involved. If someone else were the Habitat Partner, Magnolia would certainly insist upon helping too.

"All right," she said. She turned to Paddlefoot. "You, Rogo, and the Dimorphodons should remain here. If we don't return by tomorrow night, send the Dimorphodons for help. One to Volcaneum, and the other to Treetown. Those are the closest towns."

"I don't like this," Paddlefoot grumbled.

"There's no time to decide whether we like it or not," answered Magnolia. "We've come this far—we've got to know everything that's happening."

She ran over to Rogo and tried to lift the boat off the Triceratops' broad back. A second later, Birch and Aaron rushed to help her. They tied the oars inside the boat and hoisted it over their heads. They looked like a giant six-legged insect, but the three of them were able to carry the boat.

It's one thing to cart a boat over level land, thought Magnolia as they stumbled along. But she knew they still had to haul it over the bank and through the crevice in the canyon wall. Then they'd have to find a safe place to put the boat into the water. None of it was going to be easy.

As they carried the boat away, Birch gave Rogo some reassuring hoots, but the Triceratops shook his head and stamped his feet. It was strange to see two huge dinosaurs looking so worried. Even the Dimorphodons had long faces.

"Heave ho!" said Aaron as they hoisted the boat over the bank. "Be careful not to damage it!"

Magnolia swallowed hard and looked at the huge gap in the canyon. She could hear the water surging through it, and she had a feeling that the worst dangers of all still lay ahead of them.

CHAPTER 10

"Careful!" shouted Aaron over the roar of the water. "Take your time!"

Aaron, Birch, and Magnolia were attempting the impossible—carrying a boat on a narrow ledge, through a gap in a canyon wall. Below them, the water thundered over a mass of boulders, and the spray hit them in the face. To fall into that maelstrom would mean certain death.

Just walking along the ledge was hard enough, without carrying a boat. Carrying the boat meant they had to make constant adjustments in weight and balance. When one of them took a step, the others had to take a step too. And if one of them fell, thought Magnolia, the others would also fall.

Not only that, but dark shadows were creeping across the canyon, and night was only a heartbeat away. Magnolia almost ordered them to go back, thinking that this was a suicide mission. But they were halfway through the chasm, and it would be just as difficult to go backward as forward.

She marveled at the selflessness of Birch and Aaron, who were risking their lives to help her. Then again, it wasn't just her they were helping, but everyone who lived in Waterfall City.

Aaron had never even *seen* Waterfall City, and Birch had probably been there only once or twice. If they died out here in the wilderness, no one would ever know of their bravery. She had to make sure they got back safely.

Magnolia was so busy worrying that her foot slipped on the narrow ledge. "Ahh!" she screamed just as Aaron reached over and grabbed the back of her tunic. All three of them slumped back against the rock wall and tried to hold the boat steady. They panted, waiting to fall into the rapids. But no one did.

"Are you all right, missy?" asked Aaron.

She nodded and swallowed hard. "Yes. I'm sorry."

The old sailor smiled. "It's slippery up here. Just pay attention to where you step." He turned to Birch, who was in the lead. "How close are we to the end?"

"About twenty feet," said the boy. "Then we'll have solid ground to walk on."

The old man cackled. "You know it's bad when an old sailor can hardly wait to hit land."

"Thanks," breathed Magnolia, "for helping me."

"Gotta pay you folks back," said Aaron, "for making me a new man."

"Let's go," said Magnolia.

Once again, they hoisted the boat and took tiny steps across the narrow ledge. Magnolia stopped worrying and tried to concentrate on where to put her feet. It seemed to take hours, but they finally passed through the canyon and were walking on dirt, surrounded by pine trees.

"Let's set it down," said Birch wearily.

"Okay," said Magnolia. "One…two…three…go!"

With a heave, they lowered the twelve-foot boat on top of some scrawny shrubs. Magnolia's shoulders ached, and her legs were wobbly from exertion. With her sleeve, she wiped the sweat off her face and looked at the others, who were doing the same.

"I want to thank both of you," she said humbly.

"Thank us if we get back alive," answered Birch.

Magnolia took a few steps toward the surging water. In its mad rush, the water had carved a rugged channel through the forest, piling up fallen trees and bushes along its banks. There was so much debris on the bank that she had a difficult time even getting close to the new river.

As a test, Magnolia picked up a good-sized log and tossed it into the swirling water. It sunk without a trace in the rapids.

She shook her head. "We can't put the boat in here. Let's carry it a little farther downstream."

"I was about to suggest the same thing," said Aaron. He looked up at the dark sky. "Should we wait until morning?"

"No time," said Magnolia. "We still have some light left. Let's get going."

The old sailor smiled. "You'd make a good ship's captain, missy."

With weary groans, they picked up the lifeboat and started carrying it again. Now it was Birch's turn to stumble and fall, and Aaron had to hold up his end of the boat.

"Sorry," said the lad, wiping off his hands.

"Don't fret about it," Aaron told him.

They struggled through the woods, and Magnolia wished Rogo could have come with them to carve a nice path. Low-hanging tree branches brushed against the boat, making it hard to get through. Finally, Birch came to a sudden stop.

"The river widens here," he said, panting. "I think it's time to ride instead of walk."

"Sounds fine by me," muttered Aaron.

They carefully set the boat on the ground, and Magnolia went to check the water in front of them. The river widened and flowed over what looked like a meadow. The current seemed to be moving very fast, but most of the rapids were gone. Birch was right— they could put the boat in here.

She glanced up at the sky. Away from the canyon, the shadows weren't so deep, and they had maybe a half-hour of daylight left. She glanced back at Birch and Aaron. They were no more than a scrawny teenager and an old man, but they looked like heroes to her. They were waiting for her to make the decision.

"Let's go," she said.

Aaron nodded. "I've got more practice with pushing boats off than you. Let's put it into the water. I'll hold it, while the two of you jump in."

They angled the wooden boat into the swift-moving current. Aaron had to dig his feet into the mud and hold tightly to keep the boat from being swept away. Magnolia climbed in and untied the oars, and Birch moved in behind her.

When the boat began to slip away, Aaron dove in headfirst, and they were off on a wild ride!

The runaway river twirled the boat around, and the bank became nothing but a blur as it swept past. They stuck the oars into the water and tried to steer, but it was no use. The current was just too fast.

"Whaaaa!" screamed Birch as they whirled around.

"Don't look at the bank!" shouted Aaron. "It'll just make you sick!"

Magnolia decided he was right, and she stared down at her hands. The water splashed in her face as the little boat bobbed up and down in the raging river. Aaron gripped one of the oars and used it to push away logs that tried to ram them. Birch just covered his eyes and slumped into the bottom of the boat.

They plunged across the meadow and into a dark

forest, which grew even darker as nightfall descended.

When the boat finally came to rest, it was pitch black all around them. The moon was covered by clouds and offered no hint as to where they were. But Magnolia knew they had to be in a brand-new lake. Or maybe it was a swamp; it was hard to tell.

One thing was certain—this area was rapidly filling with all the water that should have been going to Waterfall City.

"Now what do we do?" asked Birch worriedly.

Aaron crawled into the stern of the little boat. "I vote for sleeping," he said.

"I guess so," agreed Magnolia. They could try to paddle to the shore, wherever that was, but what would they do once they got there? Sleep. They might as well stay with the boat and be ready to get away at first light.

The Habitat Partner was worried. If the water had kept flowing, there might have been an easy way to divert it back into its regular course. But there was no way to divert a lake. Now she knew that they would have to clear the avalanche out of the Polongo River and block up the chasm in the canyon wall.

As Paddlefoot had said, it was going to be a big job. The question was—how much time did they have?

In the darkness, there was no telling where they

were, but she suspected that they were back in the Rainy Basin. If the Rainy Basin became a huge lake, it would force the Tyrannosaurus packs to go into populated areas. That was something nobody wanted.

"Okay," she said wearily, "let's try to get some sleep. We'll need our strength for rowing tomorrow."

Suddenly, the boat began twirling around again. But they weren't going anywhere!

"Whirlpool!" shouted Magnolia. "Get the oars! We've got to get out of here!"

Aaron bolted upright from his makeshift bed and grabbed an oar. Magnolia reached for the other one, and they paddled frantically. Birch leaned over the bow of the boat and paddled with his hands.

Magnolia tried to figure out what was happening to them. All the water rushing into the new lake had nowhere to go, so it swirled into a giant whirlpool. If there was some kind of crack in the ground, it might be flowing underground.

"Row!" she shouted. "Or we'll be sucked under!"

That made them row like crazy people. After what seemed like hours, they managed to coordinate their rowing and get the boat moving in a straight line. It was a long time before they felt the jolt of land hitting the bottom of the boat.

Birch staggered ashore and tried to pull the boat with him. Magnolia splashed into the water and grabbed the side of the boat. So did Aaron. They were so tired that it took all three of them to drag the empty boat onto dry land.

They flopped onto the ground, gasping for breath. Magnolia's chest was heaving so hard it was painful.

"Get the boat," she croaked. "Bring it farther inland. Remember, this place is filling up with water."

They dragged themselves off the ground and managed to haul the boat another twenty feet. Then they collapsed again, wet and shivering, just glad to be alive. They slept where they lay, too exhausted to move.

When the first rays of sunlight struck her face, Magnolia wanted to wake up. But her weary body refused to move, and her eyelids refused to open. The sun felt so good warming her body that she just wanted to lie there, soaking it up. Forever.

Then she heard Birch say, "What do you know— look at *that!*"

Magnolia rubbed her eyes and sat up. By the stark light of day, she finally saw where they were, and she gasped with shock.

The palm trees and ferns told her they were in the Rainy Basin, but they were in a deep depression she had never seen before. She was certain she'd never seen it before, because there was a huge rock wall in front of her. On the wall were ancient reliefs—statues carved right into the rock.

The reliefs depicted scenes she had only heard about. They were scenes of the long-ago war between humans and meat eaters, such as Tyrannosaurus rex and Allosaurus. There were men spearing dinosaurs, dinosaurs eating people, and chariots chasing dinosaurs—driving them into the sea.

Magnolia thought she had seen all the historical reliefs on Dinotopia, but she had never seen these before. She had never even *heard* of them!

The carvings must have been made by humans hundreds of years ago, at the height of the war. When peace came and this area went back under the control of the meat eaters, the reliefs were forgotten. Buried deep in the Rainy Basin, home of the meat eaters, no one was likely to find them again.

Until now.

She looked with fear at the rising water. It was already at the bottom of the amazing stone carvings. In a few days, water might cover them completely!

"Do you know what we're looking at?" she asked Birch.

The boy shook his head. "I would guess these things are priceless, right?"

"Beyond priceless," she answered. "This depicts the darkest period of Dinotopia's history. These are the only firsthand reliefs of the war that have ever been found. We need to study them and learn from them. We have to *save* them."

"Is the water going to cover them?" Birch asked with alarm.

"It's going to destroy them, if we don't do something fast! Where is Aaron?"

The boy shrugged and looked around. "I don't know. Maybe he went off to look for food."

Magnolia cupped her hand to her mouth and shouted, "Aaron! Aaron! Where are you?"

In response, they heard a scream! Magnolia and Birch whirled around to look into the jungle, and they saw the old sailor running toward them. His arms were full of coconuts, which he kept dropping one by one.

"Get the boat into the water!" he yelled.

Birch laughed. "What's the matter with you?"

The smile vanished from Birch's face a moment later, when a huge Tyrannosaurus rex burst through the trees. The eighteen-foot-tall carnivore snapped his razor-sharp teeth, and his growl froze the marrow in their bones.

"*That's what!*" screamed Aaron.

CHAPTER 11

Magnolia and Birch grabbed the lifeboat and ran as if they were carrying a bag of feathers. They tossed the boat into the water and jumped aboard. Magnolia gripped a tree branch to keep the boat anchored until Aaron could get there. She wasn't sure if he would reach the boat before the Tyrannosaurus reached him.

At the last possible second, Aaron leaped headfirst into the boat, and Magnolia shoved off. The Tyrannosaurus snapped his mighty jaws inches from their heads, then he waded into the water after them.

"Row! Row!" shouted Magnolia. "Toward the whirlpool!"

No one had time to question her, as the big dinosaur used his powerful hind legs to chase after them. His huge head lunged toward the boat, and his jaws bit off a chunk of wood from the stern. Birch swung his oar and smashed the Tyrannosaurus in the snout, which caused him to pause—for only a moment.

Magnolia paddled like mad toward the whirlpool

that had nearly claimed them the night before. It was their only chance! The powerful eddy sucked the boat toward it, putting some distance between them and the hungry carnivore.

"Now row!" she screamed. "The other way!"

Aaron grabbed the oar from her, and he and Birch paddled like twin water wheels. After a few tense moments, they managed to get away from the whirlpool. As Magnolia had planned, the Tyrannosaurus wasn't so lucky. He was trying to walk on the bottom, and he lost his footing in the swift current. With his tiny forearms, he couldn't swim well, and the swirling water sucked him under.

The two men were too busy rowing to look at anything, but Magnolia turned back to look at the Tyrannosaurus. With a mighty effort, the dinosaur leaped away from the whirlpool and stumbled back to the shore. When he got back to dry land, he wiggled his forearms and growled at them.

Magnolia could feel a lump of fear in her throat. She swallowed to get rid of it.

"Can we stop rowing?" asked Aaron wearily.

"No," answered Magnolia. "We've got to get back to Paddlefoot and Rogo, and send the Dimorphodons to get help. Did you see those reliefs back there?"

"Yes," said the old sailor. "Funny place to put an art gallery."

"We've made an amazing discovery," said Magnolia. "And now we have to save it."

"Tell me," said Aaron, "are those toothy critters all over Dinotopia?"

Birch laughed. "No, they're just around here. Most people avoid the Rainy Basin."

"Whew!" said the old man. "I was beginning to think I wouldn't like it here much after all, nice as you people are."

"If you like the ocean," said Magnolia, "you could try my hometown, Sauropolis. Or if you like peace and quiet, there's a nice little fishing village called Prosperine."

"Peace and quiet sound good to me," agreed the old sailor.

They rowed the tiny lifeboat until the current in the runaway river proved too strong for them. Birch and Aaron used their last ounce of strength to row ashore. After they pulled the boat onto dry land, Magnolia looked at it sadly.

"Aaron, it's a worthy vessel," she said. "But I'm afraid we'll have to leave the boat here."

The old sailor looked sadly at his lifeboat. He reached down and ran his hand along the place where the Tyrannosaurus had taken a bite out.

"It's the only thing left from my old life," he said. "Maybe it's better to leave it here."

"You can come back to get it someday," Birch suggested.

Aaron shook his head. "Not with our toothy

friends running around here, thank you. Sometimes you have to let go of the past and move on."

Magnolia smiled at him with a tear running down her cheek.

"What's the matter, missy?"

She shrugged. "You remind me of an old friend of mine, by the name of Edwick. I hope the two of you get a chance to meet each other."

Aaron sighed and looked at the rugged forest and the rampaging river. "I hope I get a chance to meet *anybody*."

"Come on," said Magnolia. "Let's start hiking. We have to get back before sunset, before Paddlefoot and Rogo send the Dimorphodons for help. They don't know the full story."

They slogged their way through the forest, keeping a wary eye out for more meat eaters. By mid-afternoon, they reached the chasm where the water was pouring through. All Magnolia could think of was the way this water was swamping the precious reliefs. They had to stop the flow before it destroyed them!

With the spray hitting their faces, they moved slowly along the narrow ledge. It was easier to get through the chasm without carrying a boat, but it still wasn't easy. Aaron slipped on the wet rocks, and both Magnolia and Birch grabbed him before he could fall.

"I'm getting weak," said the old man. "I need to eat something."

"We all do," Magnolia agreed. "Just a little bit farther."

When she saw Paddlefoot's head peering over the fallen rocks from the avalanche, she waved frantically. She was never so glad to see the big Lambeosaurus in her entire life. Paddlefoot bellowed a sound of welcome.

"I'm glad to see you, too!" she shouted.

Forcing her weary muscles to keep working, Magnolia led the way back to the dry riverbed. Paddlefoot craned his neck toward her, and she grabbed the crest atop his head. He gently lowered her to the ground, and she rested against his chest for a moment.

Rogo stamped his feet and rushed forward to greet Birch. The thin boy hugged the Triceratops as if he would never leave him again. Aaron just slumped to the ground, catching his breath.

"We were getting very worried," honked the Lambeosaurus.

"You should still be worried," she answered. She told her friend about the amazing carvings, and how they were about to be swallowed by the runaway river.

"What can we do?" hooted the hadrosaur.

"It's all up to our little friends," answered the girl.

The two Dimorphodons sat on a fallen tree, chirping happily at the return of the humans. Magnolia walked toward them, wondering what she should tell them.

The Dimorphodons were amazing creatures—they

could remember messages in the human language and repeat them. But they also had to remember to fly to the right place to deliver the message. If Magnolia gave them too much to remember, the messages might not get through.

And they had to get through!

These were the most talented Dimorphodons in all of Waterfall City, she reminded herself. They had devoted their lives to important missions like this. Magnolia knew she could trust them.

"Bippa," she said to the female, "do you know the way to Volcaneum?"

"Yes," answered the tiny flyer. Dimorphodons didn't really speak the language of humans—they could only memorize it. But they could recognize names and cities, and they knew how to answer "yes" if they understood.

"Good," she said. "You must go to Volcaneum. This message is from the Habitat Partners of Freshwater to Tok Timbu. He must send the brachiosaurs and Triceratops—all of them—to the Polongo River at once. Follow the sound of Paddlefoot."

She paused then said, "Repeat."

The Dimorphodon cleared her throat and spoke like a parrot. "Go to Volcaneum. This message is from the Habitat Partners of Freshwater to Tok Timbu. He must send the brachiosaurs and Triceratops—all of them—to the Polongo River at once. Follow the sound of Paddlefoot."

Magnolia smiled. "Good. Fly now, little Bippa."

"Yes," answered the pterosaur importantly. Bippa spread her wings and took off toward the west. In a few seconds, she was nothing but a tiny dot over the leafy treetops of the forest. A few more seconds, and she was gone.

Magnolia turned to the male Dimorphodon and asked, "Peebo, do you know the way to Treetown?"

Peebo cocked his head puzzledly, as if he didn't quite understand.

"Treetown," Magnolia repeated.

"Yes!" he squawked. "Treetown!"

The girl smiled. "Good. You go to Treetown. This message is from the Habitat Partners of Freshwater to Norah. She must send the brachiosaurs and Triceratops—all of them—to the Polongo River at once. Follow the sound of Paddlefoot."

Magnolia paused. "Repeat."

The Dimorphodon chirped, "Peebo go to Treetown. This message is from the Habitat Partners of Freshwater to Norah. She must send the brachiosaurs and Triceratops—all of them—to the Polongo River at once. Follow the sound of Paddlefoot."

"Yes!" exclaimed Magnolia with pleasure. "Go now! Fly with the wind."

The little Dimorphodon took off in the opposite direction, toward the east. In a few seconds, he had vanished from sight over the canyon wall.

On the ground, Aaron shook his head in amazement. "Do you mean to tell me those two little parrots are going to save this crazy river?"

Magnolia smiled. "On Dinotopia, everyone contributes in the best way he or she can. On some days, the smallest creatures do the biggest jobs."

"What did you call them?" Birch asked the old man. "Parrots?"

"Well," Aaron admitted, "real parrots have feathers on them. I don't know what you folks call those featherless birds."

"They're not birds," said Magnolia. "They're pterosaurs."

The old sailor shook his head and lay back on the ground. "I don't know if I'll ever get used to this place."

Magnolia went over to her saddlebag and picked it up. "I seem to have lots of food left. Who wants some?"

"*Me!*" cried Birch and Aaron at once.

Magnolia handed out the rest of her fruits and grains, saving only a little for herself. She hoped she had done the right thing. Volcaneum and Treetown were not only the closest towns, but they had the biggest populations of Brachiosaurus nearby.

Seventy feet long, forty feet tall, and weighing 70,000 pounds on average, brachiosaurs were the biggest dinosaurs on Dinotopia. They were the mighty earth movers. They would dig the boulders out, and the Triceratops would push them. If anybody could set the Polongo River straight, it would be them.

"Paddlefoot," she said with determination. "We've got to make a plan for when a hundred brachiosaurs and Triceratops show up. What do we do first?"

The Lambeosaurus hooted. "Rogo and I were talking about that. We should clear the boulders in the riverbed first, before we divert the river. Some of those rocks we can push to the upper ridge and shove back where they came from."

"That sounds dangerous," said Magnolia. "Let's take all the safeguards we can."

Birch stepped forward and pointed to the ridge overlooking the chasm. "Rogo and the other Triceratops can push the rocks the last leg. I know how to talk to Tri-tops, so I'll supervise them." Rogo nodded his head in agreement.

Aaron rubbed his beard. "I've got a really loud whistle," said the old sailor. "It comes from working in the riggings. Maybe I can help send signals."

Magnolia nodded with relief. They would need everyone's help, but somebody had to be in charge. She knew just the one.

"Paddlefoot," said the girl, "you've got to be in charge of this project. You can talk directly to the brachiosaurs, and they can hear you over many miles. You need to direct them and tell them what to do."

The big Lambeosaurus nodded, and a gulp ran down his neck. Magnolia hugged one of his huge legs

114

and said, "We're the Habitat Partners. Everyone is looking to us to guide them. That's what Calico and Edwick would do."

Paddlefoot hooted as if to say he was ready. Magnolia stared into the sky, which had started out clear and bright. Now black clouds roiled through the blue, and the thunderheads looked very threatening toward the west.

She tried not to think about everything that was at stake. The fates of Waterfall City, the historical reliefs, the Tyrannosaurus packs, and even the Rainy Basin depended upon them, and what they did in the next few hours.

But first, it was was up to the smallest creatures of Dinotopia to summon the largest ones.

CHAPTER 12

When the cold rain began to pelt her thin body, Bippa ducked her head. The Dimorphodon swerved back and forth over the trees, trying to find warm air currents that would take away the chill and lift her higher. She didn't find any—just cold, sleeting rain, driving the heat away.

Bippa had to fly close to the branches, much closer than she liked. The big leaves looked inviting to the shivering dinosaur, but she couldn't stop to rest or get dry. She had to keep going! *Tok Timbu—send all the brachiosaurs and Triceratops to the river—save the river.*

She could remember every word the Habitat Partner had spoken, but she also understood the urgency of the mission. She had seen the river going the wrong way! It should flow south, to her home in Waterfall City. The river had strayed, and it had to be put back on course.

The Dimorphodon knew all about straying from a course. At that very moment the icy wind was buffeting her, blowing her toward the north! She had to fight to keep going due east while she searched desperately for a landmark. She looked and looked, but she couldn't see anything in the dark clouds and pouring rain!

Bippa almost bashed into a tree branch before she realized the trees were on a mountain! The mountains were an important landmark, because the city of Volcaneum was built on a crater at the southern end of the mountain range.

She flapped her wings desperately, trying to climb higher. If she didn't, she would crash into the mountains in this blinding rain! The brave Dimorphodon was soaked through and through, but she kept flapping. There would be time to rest when she completed her mission.

Now she nearly crashed into a rock wall, and she tumbled into a loop, which sent her into a tailspin. She had to flap like a demon to keep from getting caught in the trees. Finally, she got back on course and headed south with the mountain range to her right.

The lightning struck the mountains only a few yards away, blinding her with the bright light and sending her into another tailspin. This time, she let herself be forced into the trees—she didn't have enough energy to avoid it.

Bippa caught a branch with her claws and twirled around, upside down, until she finally got her balance. For several moments, the Dimorphodon just panted and shook the rain off her wings. When another lightning strike crashed nearby, she huddled under a leaf, shaking with fear and cold.

Got to go on, she told herself. *To Volcaneum—Tok Timbu—got to deliver the message.*

Bippa shook her wings and gave them a tremendous thrust, which rocketed her out between the tree branches. She flapped hard to achieve some altitude, then she realized that the lightning was attracted to the mountains. So she swerved a bit to the east, putting some distance between herself and the mountain range.

It took a lot of wing power, but she finally outran the storm. Then she had a new worry—the sun was sinking on the other side of the mountains. She didn't want to fly near a mountain in darkness and rain, so she beat her wings all the harder.

Bippa strained her neck to find some sign of Volcaneum on the ragged horizon of the mountains. Finally, she saw the glow, like a candlewick on top of a pudding, and she set aim for the city built on top of the dormant volcano.

Her wings were numb from exertion by the time she swerved over the quaint houses of the city. They were built like colorful steps around the sides of the crater. She was looking for the glow of the forges— that was the place for a master metalworker such as Tok Timbu.

She was spotted before she could find the foundry.

A lamplighter who was plying his trade atop a Deinocheirus waved to the pterosaur.

"Message carrier! Rest here a moment!" he called. He doused the wick on his lamp rod and set it down to make a perch across his saddle.

Utterly exhausted, the Dimorphodon went into a slow spiral and tried not to crash-land into the big dinosaur. She came close to the perch, but the lamplighter had to catch her.

"Poor thing," he muttered. "You've come far, and in the rain. Who are you seeking?"

"Tok Timbu!" she squeaked. She wondered if she should repeat all of the message.

"Save your energy," insisted the lamplighter. "I will take you to Tok Timbu straightaway."

Norah looked at the pile of dirty laundry and at the pile of vegetables and walnuts, that needed to be sliced and cracked. She wondered which pile she should tackle first. As she looked closer, she realized she shouldn't have to tackle the laundry at all, because most of it belonged to her visiting nephew, Douglas.

"Douglas!" she called. As Norah had expected, there was no answer, and she had to lean out the window of the treehouse. She had a good view, which was one of the reasons she lived in the heights, sixty feet from the ground. And Norah knew exactly where to look for visiting nephews.

Even though it was getting dark, Douglas was at

the swimming hole with some local children. They were swinging from a vine and trying to land on an Apatosaurus's back. If they made it, the dinosaur's tail became a slide. As they got better at the game, the Apatosaurus moved a few feet to make it harder. The dinosaur stood hip-deep in the water, so the children got safely dunked no matter where they landed.

That was the only trouble with Treetown, thought Norah—it was just too much fun for visiting youngsters. No wonder all of his clothes were filthy.

Douglas had just climbed out of the water and was headed back up the ladder for another try. "Douglas!" she called sharply.

The twelve-year-old stopped and looked up at her, grinning sheepishly. He knew he had been playing nonstop for three days. "Yes, Aunt Norah?"

"You know the rules," said the gray-haired lady. "All boys do their own laundry. The way you've been playing, you've gotten every stitch you own dirty!"

"Go on!" shouted one of the other boys. "It's getting dark, anyway. We'll see you tomorrow!"

They all started scampering away, and one of them waved back. "Hi, Aunt Norah!"

She pretended to frown. "I'm not *your* aunt, Peter, just Douglas's. Is *your* laundry done?"

"Sure thing!" Peter called back. Then something caught his eye. He pointed excitedly. "Look, Norah! A messenger!"

Norah followed his finger and saw a little Dimorphodon swerving erratically through the leafy boughs. It was headed right for her, but she waved, anyway.

"Over here! Over here!" She opened her window all the way to give him the entire windowsill as a perch.

Peebo wobbled in for a landing, looking beaten and half-drowned. He just sat on the windowsill, shivering. No one would send a Dimorphodon on a flight like that, reasoned Norah, unless it was an emergency.

She gently placed a clean dish towel around his scrawny shoulders for warmth and let him collect his wits.

"They call you Norah?" he chirped. "Norah?"

She nodded somberly. "Yes, I am Norah."

The Dimorphodon nodded with satisfaction. "This message is from the Habitat Partners of Freshwater to Norah. She must send the brachiosaurs and Triceratops—all of them—to the Polongo River at once. Follow the sound of Paddlefoot."

The older lady gasped and put her hand to her mouth. She had seen the messages on the crystal beacon—this was the call to action. The Polongo River and Waterfall City must be seriously threatened!

Norah took the little pterosaur and rested him on the back of her favorite rocking chair. "You have done well," she told him. "In a moment, I'll fix you some broth. First, business."

The matriarch of Treetown leaned out of her window again. The boys had watched with rapt attention as she spoke to the messenger, and now they weren't going to move until they found out what had happened.

"You children!" she shouted. "Find every horn blower in the town and countryside. Tell them to call the brachiosaurs and Triceratops! We will meet in the meadow. Hurry!"

About a hundred miles away, a muscular man listened to the same message. As he nodded, his bald head glistened in the reddish light cast off by the forge. When Bippa was finished with her message, Tok Timbu patted the Dimorphodon's scaly head and gave her a sip of his tea.

He stood up and grabbed a gigantic rod of steel that was nearly as long as his arm. He slapped it into his fist, then he began to climb up an old wooden ladder.

There was a bell tower at the top of Tok's foundry. It wasn't used very often, but it contained the loudest bell he had ever made—forged from bronze that had since turned green. People joked and said they heard complaints from the graveyard when he rang that bell.

As the wooden ladder creaked under his weight, Tok Timbu thought about the signal he would have to ring. To call all the brachiosaurs and Triceratops within hearing—that was a command not given lightly. This must be a major undertaking to need so many earth movers.

He hoped the new Habitat Partners knew what they were doing.

A strong wind whipped through the bell tower, and Tok Timbu took some cotton from the pocket of his apron. He stuffed the cotton in his ears and charged up the final steps.

Tok planted his feet as the wind swirled around him. Then he swung the iron rod with all his might, striking the bell and producing a thunderous tone that engulfed him. He could feel the vibrations all the way to his teeth. He swiftly swung again three times. He paused and ended the message with one long, deafening bong.

That night all over Dinotopia, horns and bells were sounded. Every Brachiosaurus and Triceratops within hearing rousted himself from a lazy bog or a warm barn. The giants plowed through swamps and thickets, across mountains and plains. The ground shook that night as the earth movers formed mighty herds.

Norah, Tok Timbu, and the other humans lit their lamps to guide the way through town and field. They studied their maps and showed the dinosaurs the quickest routes. A few brave humans offered to ride along, to carry lanterns.

But the dinosaurs didn't need any lanterns or

maps after they heard Paddlefoot's plaintive hoot. It was like a loon call on the lake, but it stretched over the miles, over the mountains, and into the senses of every Brachiosaurus and Triceratops.

After they heard Paddlefoot's call, they ran toward the sound. Nothing could stop the brachiosaurs; they were the mightiest force on Dinotopia.

All night long, they tromped through the Rainy Basin, and even the tyrannosaurs stayed out of their way.

CHAPTER 13

Birch jumped to his feet. "Do you feel it?" he asked excitedly.

In the quiet moments just before dawn, only the skinny lad and Paddlefoot were awake. Paddlefoot nodded, then he cut loose with a mournful bellow. The sound echoed from the resonating chamber on the top of his head and floated over the treetops.

They were downriver some distance from Magnolia, Aaron, and Rogo, who were all asleep. Paddlefoot could not sleep, because he had to call the brachiosaurs. All night long, his companions took turns keeping him company, and it was Birch's turn.

"They're coming—do you feel it?" shouted Birch. "The ground is shaking!" He lay down in the riverbed and put his ear to the sand. "There must be hundreds of them! I never thought I'd see a sight like this."

Birch jumped up and smiled at Paddlefoot. "You're doing a great job—keep it up! I'll go wake the others." He ran off, flapping his arms like a scarecrow.

Paddlefoot snorted a laugh, then returned to his resonant calls.

An hour later, the sunlight was creeping over the canyon into the dry riverbed, and the noise of the approaching dinosaurs was deafening! Magnolia, Birch, and Aaron waited tensely as seventy-foot-long dinosaurs thundered closer. Their heads snaked over the treetops, like periscopes in a sea of leaves.

"We're going up on the ridge!" shouted Birch over the noise. He jumped onto Rogo's back, and they climbed over the riverbank, headed toward the chasm.

Aaron seemed to be shivering, but it was just the ground shaking under him. "Blimey, what a sight!" he croaked. He stared in amazement as the line of brachiosaurs, each standing forty feet tall, burst through the trees. The Triceratops were not far behind them.

Magnolia swallowed. They all knew their duties in this matter—they knew what was supposed to happen. They had worked it out with Paddlefoot the night before. But now that the great earth movers were upon them, the girl's mind had gone blank.

Of course, Paddlefoot remembered what he was supposed to do. The Lambeosaurus waved his tail at the boulders blocking the river. Then he pointed toward the V-shaped chasm in the canyon wall. The brachiosaurs craned their long necks to see the water pounding into this new channel, away from the river's true course.

Paddlefoot hooted several commands through his crest, and the earth movers grew still and listened. They were pouring out of the woods on both sides of the river now, and Magnolia could only gape in awe.

Paddlefoot was very graceful, and he made it clear from his movements and accompanying hoots exactly what he wanted done. Then he looked at the humans and snorted, basically telling them to get out of the way.

Magnolia grabbed Aaron. "You're good at climbing trees," she said. "We need to get high up to get an overview of the river."

The old sailor looked relieved to get away from the giant sauropods. He and Magnolia scrambled up the bank and found the tallest palm tree in the area. They climbed up in time to see the end of Paddle-foot's instructions.

Their timing had been good, thought Magnolia. The sky was clear, and it looked as if it would stay that way until the afternoon. They had a whole day of work ahead of them.

Paddlefoot bellowed, and the first wave of earth movers lumbered into the riverbed. The ones on the west bank, from Volcaneum, went straight toward the boulders plugging up the river. The ones on the east, from Treetown, formed a chain that led up the bank toward the ridge overlooking the chasm.

Magnolia could just make out Birch and Rogo at the top of the ridge. An angry flood of water coursed through the gap beneath them. She hoped they would be careful! They had the last and most crucial job—seeing that the boulders were dropped into the chasm where the water was escaping.

She shook her head. In the end, the success of this whole endeavor depended upon two bored farmers who were looking for adventure.

Paddlefoot hooted again, and the brachiosaurs straddled the boulders in the riverbed. Like giant dogs digging holes, they used their massive front legs to uproot the rocks and move them backward. The debris from the avalanche began to move, and some of the smaller rocks fell down and bounced along the dry riverbed.

The Triceratops downstream caught the boulders and pushed them up the riverbank with their armored heads. Using their necks and heads like power shovels, the earth movers pushed the boulders along the line. Their destination was the top of the ridge, where Rogo and Birch waited.

Pushing heavy rocks uphill was much slower work than digging them out. But slow and steady was fine with Magnolia. They had to get the riverbank entirely cleared before they started to dam up the gorge. No one knew how all that water would react, and it could be dangerous.

It was her job to tell them when the time was right to turn the river back.

Aaron gave a low whistle as he surveyed the amazing scene. "This here is incredible. Those critters are like islands with legs on them!"

Magnolia chuckled. "That's a good way to put it." She grew somber. "It all depends on Birch and Rogo."

The sailor nodded. "I know. Don't worry about them, missy. They know what they're doing."

The girl turned her attention back to the amazing activity in the riverbed. It wasn't frenzied activity—it was slow, grinding, earth-moving activity. On the more stubborn boulders, the brachiosaurs teamed up. They smashed big stones together to make them smaller and easier to move.

There was also a lot of smaller debris, such as fallen trees. Magnolia pointed to a clearing on the bank where the debris could be stored, and the Triceratops began to move the logs.

Under Paddlefoot's direction, the earth movers pushed hundreds of boulders over the riverbed. Then another line of Triceratops took over and pushed the boulders, inch by inch, up the ridge. Their grunts and groans echoed through the Rainy Basin.

Each Triceratops was in charge of one boulder, and he held it on the ridge until the signal was given. At the top of the ridge, overlooking the runaway rapids, Rogo waited to push the first boulder into the chasm. The Triceratops was so anxious that he was stomping his feet.

Magnolia had to decide when the river was clear enough to begin the second phase. She was worried about the danger of all that rushing water suddenly changing direction. She was also worried about the boulders the Triceratops would be pushing—if they fell the wrong way, they could do more harm than good.

She wanted to be cautious, but time was running out for Waterfall City and the precious reliefs in the jungle. Turning back a river was not a job for the fainthearted.

Magnolia waved to Paddlefoot, but he couldn't see her. That was when Aaron stuck his fingers in his mouth and cut loose with a seaman's whistle that was deafening. A second later, Magnolia had the attention of Paddlefoot, Rogo, and all the other dinosaurs.

"Move them out of the river!" she called down to Paddlefoot. "It's cleared enough!"

As Paddlefoot bellowed, the brachiosaurs in the riverbed began to move out. The Triceratops on the canyon side stepped up their efforts to push the rocks uphill. They grunted and stomped, and the rocks kept moving.

Aaron shook his head in wonder. "Without those dinosaurs," he said, "a job like this would take humans months, maybe years, to pull off."

"That could be," Magnolia answered. "Luckily,

I've never had to live without dinosaurs."

Within a few seconds, Paddlefoot and the brachiosaurs had vacated the riverbed. Everyone was looking at Magnolia again, and she waved to Rogo.

"Drop the rocks!" she shouted.

The Triceratops leaned forward, and his massive legs stiffened. Slowly the boulder began to scoot toward the gaping gorge. Rogo's feet pawed the ground, and he started to pick up speed. Magnolia caught her breath, hoping he could stop himself before he got to the drop-off!

The Triceratops thundered toward the edge. At the last second, he planted his feet and tossed his massive head. The boulder actually bounced away from him and hurtled deep into the chasm. It hit the rapids with a huge splash! Water streamed all around it, and some of it rushed back into the old riverbed.

"Perfect shot!" shouted Magnolia with excitement. That was only the first of many perfect shots they would need.

But Birch was already directing the next Triceratops in line, and he thundered toward the gorge and tossed another boulder into the maelstrom. With amazing efficiency, each Triceratops did the same, then they rushed down to get another boulder.

Birch never seemed to tire as he waved his hands and growled and grunted. Each Triceratops snorted with pride as his rock plummeted into the chasm. Magnolia was counting, and it was the forty-fifth stone that turned the tide. That big chunk of granite pounded down on top of all the others and flattened them into a dam.

The water swerved an instant later, rushing up over the banks and splashing the brachiosaurs. Then the raging water smashed through what was left of the dam in the river. And the Polongo River flowed again!

Dinosaurs bellowed, and the few people on hand cheered. Still, the work wasn't over. Rogo and his brethren had many more boulders to drop into the chasm to cement their work. The brachiosaurs set to work repairing the riverbanks, keeping the river flowing where it should.

Magnolia peered into the distance. From atop the palm tree, she could see some of the second river and the lake it formed in the Rainy Basin. She couldn't see the water level dropping in the lake—it would be too soon for that—but she could see the level dropping in the channel!

Aaron slapped her on the back and nearly knocked her out of the tree. "You've won!" he crowed. "You put the river true again! Oh, I wish I had my boat to take off on that lovely current."

Magnolia nodded wearily. She wished they had Aaron's boat, too, as they could reach Waterfall City in a matter of hours by boat. Instead they faced two or three days of walking through the jungle, not a leisurely stroll down a dry riverbed.

Then Magnolia grinned. The riverbed wasn't dry

anymore! It was covered with roiling, dirty water, and it looked beautiful! She tried to calm down, reminding herself that the job wasn't done yet. She could see how hard the brachiosaurs, the Triceratops, and Birch were still working.

But the Polongo River was running true again. She and Paddlefoot had succeeded in their first mission as the Habitat Partners.

She waved to Paddlefoot and shook her fist in victory. The Lambeosaurus bellowed his loudest cry yet, and the joyful noise floated over the treetops.

The earth movers worked until late afternoon before they were fully satisfied with their work. Once they had dropped as many rocks as they could into the chasm, the brachiosaurs sealed it with mud and stomped it down with their feet. They were intent upon making the canyon as good as new, as it was before the earthquake and the avalanche.

Magnolia finally knew that the earth movers were done when the herds turned in unison and lumbered back into the forest. They were in no hurry, and they paid careful attention to where they walked. A few of the brachiosaurs had to ford the river, where they moved gracefully through the surging water.

They were islands with legs, as Aaron had called them. The old sailor was asleep under a palm tree, felled by all the excitement, and Magnolia decided to let him rest.

Rogo was lying down, as well he should, and Birch was rubbing ointment on his cuts and bruises. Even a Triceratops got bruises when he pushed boulders around all day.

Magnolia bent down and helped massage the salve into his thick hide. "Wonderful job you did, Rogo. You too, Birch. We couldn't have done it without you, and that's a fact."

"Yeah," said Birch glumly.

"What's the matter?" asked Magnolia. "Aren't you happy? We turned back the river and made it run true. And you two were the heroes!"

The Triceratops gave her a weary snuffle.

Birch shrugged. "Yeah, we did it all right. That was great—it worked just as we planned. But now the adventure's over, and we don't know what's going to happen to us."

Rogo groaned, and Birch added, "You guys get to do stuff like this every day."

Magnolia shook her head in disbelief. "We *don't* do this every day. I've been an apprentice for five years, and we've *never* done this before! I hope we never do it again."

"You know what I mean," grumbled Birch.

Magnolia looked at Paddlefoot, but the big hadrosaur didn't have any answers either.

"I can't give you career advice," said Magnolia, "but why don't you come back to Waterfall City with us? Aaron is going to come with us. I'd like to tell everyone what a great job you did here. I want them to meet you."

Birch perked up a little bit. "Really?" he asked.

"Sure," answered Magnolia, "and we need Rogo to protect us from tyrannosaurs." She winked at Paddle-foot.

The Triceratops sniffed, as if that was certainly the truth.

CHAPTER 14

The next two days were uneventful as the tiny band slogged their way through the Rainy Basin. Aaron rode on Paddlefoot for a while and was delighted. Rogo and Birch mainly kept to themselves. They were a lot less jolly now that the quest was over, thought Magnolia.

The group tried to keep close to the Polongo River, but the river wound back and forth so much that it was better to go in a straight line. Rogo plowed the way as usual. Since they weren't in any hurry, they stopped often to collect food, which kept everyone's spirits up.

Magnolia had a feeling that the Tyrannosaurus had spread the word to leave them alone. They never saw so much as a footprint.

They were still a day's journey away from Waterfall City when they met up with an old friend. Bippa came swooping over the river, squawking cheerfully. Magnolia and Birch waved, and the Dimorphodon landed on her usual perch, at the tip of Rogo's horn.

"How are you, Bippa?" Magnolia asked happily. "Do you have a message for us?"

The Dimorphodon nodded importantly. "A message from Malik to the Habitat Partners of Freshwater. Thank you! Thank you! Thank you! The Polongo River flows, the Spiral Clock turns, and all is well with Waterfall City. The populace is awaiting your arrival. There will be a parade in your honor."

Aaron laughed and slapped his leg. "They don't do things halfway here, do they? A parade in your honor!"

Magnolia sighed. "On Dinotopia, you don't need much excuse to hold a parade. The sun coming up is usually reason enough."

She didn't want a lot of celebration just for doing her job. Then she remembered that the parade was really more for the return of the Polongo River. That was a major event to the people of Waterfall City.

Birch asked, "Did they say anything about Rogo and me?"

The Dimorphodon cocked her head puzzledly. Finally she chirped, "Sorry."

"Don't you see, lad," said Aaron, "they don't know about you, me, and Rogo. They'll know us just fine after they meet us."

"That's right," agreed Magnolia. "All they know is that they sent Paddlefoot and me out several days ago, and now the river has returned. We've got a lot to tell them."

She motioned to Bippa. "Can you take a message back to Malik?"

"Yes," squawked the Dimorphodon.

"Tell him that our work is not yet finished. There are important historical reliefs hidden in the Rainy Basin, where the new lake formed. We must assemble a team to study them, and negotiate with the tyrannosaurs. Repeat."

The small pterosaur repeated the message and took off without further bidding. Magnolia watched her go, then smiled.

Birch frowned and patted Rogo's thick neck. "Maybe we should go back to farming. We can get another crop in before the first frost. With all this water around, maybe we should try rice."

Rogo snorted and trotted ahead of the others.

Aaron clicked his tongue and said, "Missy, you should've mentioned the two of them when you sent back that report."

"Oh no," Magnolia groaned as she watched Birch and Rogo ride off. "You're right, I should have. I know about the ways of water, but not too much about people."

"You'd better start learning right away," growled Aaron. "You've got an important job, so the way you treat people means something."

Magnolia nodded glumly. A parade in her honor, someone being hurt because she forgot to say something, accolades for her when others had done more work—she wasn't prepared for this side of being a Habitat Partner.

She tapped Paddlefoot, who shook himself awake under her. "What?" he hooted. "We were stopped, so can't a fellow take a nap?"

"Could you please catch up with Birch and Rogo? I've got to talk with them."

Paddlefoot nodded and whirled around gracefully, for a creature who weighed several tons. He trotted after Birch and Rogo, but the Triceratops sped up when he saw them coming.

"Forget it," she said, and Paddlefoot trotted to a stop. "If they want to be stubborn, let them."

Magnolia began to hope that the celebration on her return to Waterfall City would be a small affair. Maybe they had been parading around for days, she thought, and they were all tired out

No such luck.

Before they even reached the city itself, they could see hundreds of people and dinosaurs lining the northern cliffs. They began cheering as soon as the tiny band was in sight. Rogo and Birch fell back and let Magnolia and Paddlefoot take the lead. She wanted to protest, but when the crowd saw her they went wild with cheering.

They could see the distant walls of Waterfall City, surrounded by turquoise water and magical mists. That glorious sight would have been reward enough for Magnolia, but it wasn't enough for the grateful Dinotopians. A squadron of horn blowers sounded a stirring fanfare, and dinosaur heads popped up like periscopes. The tromping of dinosaur feet signaled the start of the parade.

A sea of colorful banners, ribbons, and costumes greeted Magnolia and Paddlefoot. The parade flowed through the streets of the village that overlooked Waterfall City. There were giant paper dragons, dinosaurs festooned with bright tapestries, jugglers and acrobats, and clowns riding wooden dinosaurs. It was like all the festivals rolled into one!

Magnolia looked back to find Rogo, Birch, and Aaron, but the crowd was closing in around them. She thought she caught Aaron waving to her, but the old man was on foot and got swallowed up in the joyful crowd.

Paddlefoot struggled nobly through the madness, and they soon found themselves at the head of the parade. Now the horn blowers began a loud and stirring march, and a cadre of drummers joined in. Several hadrosaurs hooted in perfect harmony as a tribute to Paddlefoot.

When they rounded a corner of the street, the crowd in the village square went crazy. Children showered Magnolia and Paddlefoot with blossoms and garlands. It was embarrassing! But the Habitat Partners plunged gamely on, with Magnolia waving and smiling to the blissful citizens.

Where were Rogo and Birch? she wondered. And Aaron? She looked around and saw that it would have been impossible for them to keep up with her. Hundreds of gaily decorated dinosaurs, floats, and marchers had fallen in behind them.

No quicksand, rapids, or tyrannosaurs could separate her from her comrades, but a crowd of people had done it in a second.

Magnolia almost wanted to go look for them, but she couldn't leave the parade. The citizens of Waterfall City had suffered a lot during the days when the fate of their river was unknown. They deserved to have their celebration, and she was part of it.

Her smile was fading as they rounded the last street corner, then Magnolia saw something that made her squeal with delight. A viewing stand had been erected at the end of the parade route, and in this place of honor sat her parents and Edwick, her old master.

"Mother! Father!" shouted Magnolia with happiness.

"That's our daughter!" yelled her father. "The Habitat Partner of Freshwater!" Everyone within earshot cheered the proud parents, who had come all the way from Sauropolis.

Magnolia looked at Edwick, the man she still considered to be the *real* Habitat Partner. He looked as fit as she had ever seen him! He must have made a wonderful recovery from the burns he had suffered. Magnolia was glad that she had been able to give him time to rest, to heal.

Edwick nodded to her and held up his fist in triumph. He was so happy that he had to dab a handkerchief at his eyes.

Several dinosaur dignitaries sat near her parents and Edwick, including Bix, a Protoceratops who was hardly bigger than a calf. Nevertheless, Bix was an ambassador and was well known all over Dinotopia.

Calico stood beside the viewing stand. The proud Saltasaurus trumpeted a welcome to her former apprentice, Paddlefoot.

After the noise died down, Bix rose up on a special podium designed just for her. "Bring the heroes forward!" she honked. "Before all of Dinotopia, we recognize the Habitat Partners of Freshwater! Paddlefoot and Magnolia!"

The cheers, hoots, and horns were deafening. It sounded as if every creature in Waterfall City was trying to outdo the others in making the most noise.

When they quieted down, Bix said, "They have never had a proper swearing-in—there wasn't time. As their first order of business, they had to capture the Polongo River and send it home!"

Now the noise doubled, and Magnolia thought she would faint. She gripped Paddlefoot's neck, hoping she wouldn't fall off before Bix's speech was over.

But the small Protoceratops had only one thing more to say: "Generations to come will remember this day. Not because the river was saved, but because this was the day when Paddlefoot and Magnolia truly became the Habitat Partners of Freshwater. May their service to Dinotopia be long and peaceful!"

With her parents and Edwick leading the cheers, the crowd went crazy. The dinosaurs stomped their feet, and people threw their hats and plumes high in the air!

Birch and Rogo were still standing at the path that led north into the forest. They watched in awe as the parade moved away from them. Bringing up the rear were a bunch of stilt-walkers in colorful costumes— they even towered over the dinosaurs! The whole thing was an amazing spectacle, the likes of which Birch had never seen and never expected to see again.

He patted Rogo on the head. "At least we got to see some awesome sights, didn't we? I guess we can't complain too much."

Rogo snorted, as if he *could* complain if he wanted to.

Birch sighed. "Of course, we left our fields half-planted. We really ought to go back and finish the job. If the birds left us any seeds, that is."

Rogo groaned in agreement. Most of the crowd was following the parade, so there was plenty of room for the big Triceratops to turn around. Slowly, he headed down the path leading out of town.

"Whoa there!" called a voice. Birch turned to see

Aaron running toward him. "Where are you two going?" he demanded.

"Back to our farm," muttered Birch. "Can't you see? Playtime is over—at least for us. We've got real life to get back to, not this."

"This is real life!" the old sailor insisted. "Let's stick around and find Magnolia. I'm sure she wants to tell everyone what you did."

"No," said Birch, shaking his head. "They've got their heroes and their parade. That's part of Magnolia's job, not mine. Where are you going from here?"

The old sailor scratched his chin. "Well, the more I hear about Prosperine, the better I like it. They've got a saltwater channel there, and the fishing is supposed to be good. Maybe they could use a few pointers from a fellow who's been on the high seas."

"Sounds good," said Birch. "I hope you have success at it. Come on, Rogo." The big Triceratops marched off, away from the rest of the parade.

The little man ran after him. "Wait! I'm sure the people here want to meet you!"

But Rogo and Birch were already in the forest, leaving the noise and the cheering behind them.

The lad stroked his friend's thick hide. "You know, Rogo, maybe we should go back to the farm where we were raised. There aren't any parades there, but the farmers know us and like us. I'm lonely living by ourselves. What do you say?"

The Triceratops grunted in agreement, and they

rode slowly down the trail. After a while, they couldn't even see the city behind them, but they could still hear the noise of the parade. It was funny, but no matter how far they rode, the sound of merrymaking did not seem to go away.

"Those people just keep getting louder and louder," Birch complained. "Don't they ever quit?"

Rogo stopped suddenly, as if something was wrong. He sniffed the air and turned around.

"What is it, boy?" asked Birch with concern. "Is somebody behind us?"

Birch expected to see a Tyrannosaurus, but he wasn't aware of any tyrannosaurs that played the drums. As they listened to what was usually a quiet forest, the sounds of drumming and horns just kept getting louder and louder.

"This is crazy," said Birch. "What are those city-folk doing?"

Rogo snorted and pawed the ground. He braced himself to charge against their attackers. Then they saw them swaying over the trees—humans walking on stilts! Behind them came the drummers, the horn blowers, the dinosaurs, the jugglers, the acrobats, and the children throwing flowers.

"What the...?"

Birch blinked in amazement at the wondrous sight, and Rogo snorted with alarm. The whole parade had turned around and was following them into the forest! As the parade came closer, it was clear that everyone was looking at them!

Rogo grunted and shook his head.

"Yeah," muttered Birch. "If I didn't know better, I'd say this parade was for *us!*"

A familiar figure bounded to the front of the merrymakers. It was Paddlefoot, with Magnolia and Aaron riding on his back! Then came a Saltasaurus with an old man riding her, and a regal wagon, carrying a Protoceratops and people he didn't know.

Magnolia grinned at him. "You don't get away from the gratitude of Waterfall City that easily. You shared the danger, and now you have to share the celebration! We couldn't have saved the river without them—Rogo and Birch!"

The joyful crowd cheered so loudly that the forest trembled, and birds bolted from the trees. That night the party spread all over Dinotopia, and there was a huge feast in honor of the brave band who brought the Polongo River back to life.